— .✦. —

PRAISE FOR DONNA GRANT'S
BEST-SELLING ROMANCE NOVELS

— .✦. —

"Grant's ability to quickly convey complicated
backstory makes this jam-packed love story accessible
even to new or periodic readers."
–Publishers' Weekly

"Donna Grant has given the paranormal genre
a burst of fresh air…"
–San Francisco Book Review

"The premise is dramatic and heartbreaking; the characters are
colorful and engaging; the romance is spirited and seductive."
–The Reading Cafe

"The central romance, fueled by a hostage drama, plays
out in glorious detail against a backdrop of multiple ongoing
issues in the "Dark Kings" books. This seemingly penultimate
installment creates a nice segue to a climactic end."
–Library Journal

"…intense romance amid the growing
war between the Dragons and the
Dark Fae is scorching hot."
–Booklist

DRAGON KINGS® SERIES

Dragon Revealed ~ Dragon Mine

Dragon Unbound ~ Dragon Eternal

Dragon Lover ~ Dragon Arisen

Dragon Frost ~ Dragon Kiss ~ Dragon Born

Dragon Marked ~ Dragon Forged ~ Dragon Sieged

SKYE DRUIDS SERIES

Iron Ember ~ Shoulder the Skye ~ Heart of Glass

Endless Skye ~ Still of the Night ~ Blood Skye

After Midnight ~ Kiss of Skye

DARK KINGS SERIES

Dark Heat ~ Darkest Flame ~ Fire Rising

Burning Desire ~ Hot Blooded ~ Night's Blaze

Soul Scorched ~ Dragon King ~ Passion Ignites

Smoldering Hunger ~ Smoke and Fire

Dragon Fever ~ Firestorm ~ Blaze ~ Dragon Burn

Constantine: A History, Parts 1-3 ~ Heat ~ Torched

Dragon Night ~ Dragonfire ~ Dragon Claimed

Ignite ~ Fever ~ Dragon Lost ~ Flame ~ Inferno

A Dragon's Tale (Whisky and Wishes: *A Holiday Novella*,

Heart of Gold: *A Valentine's Novella*, and

Of Fire and Flame) ~ My Fiery Valentine

The Dragon King Coloring Book

Dragon King Special Edition

Character Coloring Book: Rhi

DARK WARRIORS SERIES
Midnight's Master ~ Midnight's Lover
Midnight's Seduction ~ Midnight's Warrior
Midnight's Kiss ~ Midnight's Captive
Midnight's Temptation ~ Midnight's Promise
Midnight's Surrender ~ A Warrior for Christmas

CHIASSON SERIES
Wild Fever ~ Wild Dream ~ Wild Need
Wild Flame ~ Wild Rapture

LARUE SERIES
Moon Kissed ~ Moon Thrall
Moon Struck ~ Moon Bound

WICKED TREASURES
Seized by Passion ~ Enticed by Ecstasy ~ Captured by Desire

✦

HISTORICAL PARANORMAL

THE KINDRED SERIES
Everkin ~ Eversong ~ Everwylde
Everbound ~ Evernight ~ Everspell

KINDRED: THE FATED SERIES
Rage ~ Ruin ~ Reign

DARK SWORD SERIES
Dangerous Highlander
Forbidden Highlander ~ Wicked Highlander
Untamed Highlander ~ Shadow Highlander
Darkest Highlander

ROGUES OF SCOTLAND SERIES
The Craving ~ The Hunger
The Tempted ~ The Seduced

THE SHIELDS SERIES
A Dark Guardian ~ A Kind of Magic
A Dark Seduction ~ A Forbidden Temptation ~ A Warrior's Heart
Mystic Trinity (a series connecting novel)

DRUIDS GLEN SERIES
Highland Mist ~ Highland Nights ~ Highland Dawn
Highland Fires ~ Highland Magic
Mystic Trinity (a series connecting novel)

SISTERS OF MAGIC TRILOGY
Shadow Magic ~ Echoes of Magic ~ Dangerous Magic

**THE ROYAL CHRONICLES
NOVELLA SERIES**
Prince of Desire ~ Prince of Seduction
Prince of Love ~ Prince of Passion
Mystic Trinity
(a series connecting novel)

COWBOY/
CONTEMPORARY

HEART OF TEXAS SERIES
The Christmas Cowboy Hero
Cowboy, Cross My Heart ~ My Favorite Cowboy
A Cowboy Like You ~ Looking for a Cowboy
A Cowboy Kind of Love

✦

MILITARY ROMANCE/ROMANTIC SUSPENSE

SONS OF TEXAS SERIES
The Hero ~ The Protector ~ The Legend
The Defender ~ The Guardian

✦

STAND ALONE BOOKS
That Cowboy of Mine ~ Home for a Cowboy Christmas
Mutual Desire ~ Forever Mine ~ Savage Moon

✦

**Check out Donna Grant's Online Store at
www.DonnaGrant.com/shop
for autographed books, character
themed goodies, and more!**

Dark Alpha's Lover

NEW YORK TIMES & USA TODAY BESTSELLING AUTHOR

DONNA GRANT

DARK ALPHA'S LOVER

THE REAPERS

The seven there are, warriors all.
Do not do wrong or their blade will fall.
Their appearances shrouded.
Their approach, clouded.
Against evil they fight.
Power and magic are their might.
They serve only one.
If you expose their identity – run.
Secrecy is their defense.
If the truth escapes, Death will commence.

CHAPTER

one

Galway, Ireland
January

Nothing was ever as it seemed.

There were more than humans walking this earth. The things seen out of the corner of your eye were real, even if your mind refused to recognize—or accept—them.

But Catriona Hayes knew of their existence, even if she wished she didn't. They were Fae. Magical creatures that were so beautiful they seemed otherworldly—because they were.

The Fae had come to this world, seamlessly integrating themselves into the lives of mortals. But then again, when it came to beings with magic, they could do such things.

Cat blew out a breath and put the day's earnings in the pouch before placing it inside the safe and shutting the door. She straightened and looked through the windows of the café and across the street to the pub alight with merriment.

There was a bit of wistfulness within her when she spotted three women walking into the bar with bright smiles. She'd never been that carefree.

From the first moment she could remember, her family had kept her apart from others. It wasn't until she was older that she realized what made her so different—she was a Halfling.

Part human, part Fae.

Some might rejoice at the news, but she wasn't most people.

The first time her grandfather had told her of her heritage, she'd laughed, thinking it was a jest. But as they'd walked down the streets of Galway, he began pointing out the Fae.

That was the day her life changed. At eight years old, she'd felt the weight of the world drop upon her shoulders. The burden had nearly brought her to her knees. And it had lingered, growing heavier with each passing year.

Yet she remained standing beneath it all. Only because of her grandfather. The man who smiled in the midst of the many storms life threw his way. He was what kept her composed and mindful of the dangers of living near Fae.

While she had been fearful of her grandfather's revelation, her older siblings had embraced it as a gift.

Cat looked down at the counter and the top that covered it. Beneath the thick glass, next to the register, was a picture of her with her brother and sister twenty years ago.

Whatever gift having Fae blood had given her siblings had been taken away in a cruel twist of Fate several months ago when they were savagely killed.

Her brother had been murdered in a crowded pub, while her sister had had her life snuffed out on a train to London. No one had seen either attack. One moment, her siblings had been alive.

The next, they were dead. It was how Cat knew the Fae were responsible.

Only beings with magic and the ability to veil themselves could have committed such crimes without a single person catching something on their mobile phones.

Ever since her family's deaths, she'd been waiting for the Fae to come for her.

What was taking them so long? She and her grandfather—who she kept locked safely away in his cottage where no Fae could enter—were the only ones left.

A flash of lightning pulled her from her thoughts and reminded her that she needed to get home. She started toward the front, turning off the lights as she went. Flipping the sign in the café window to CLOSED, she walked out the door and locked it.

When she faced the street once more, she gripped the handle of her purse and looked around at the people. She knew the Fae could use glamour to disguise themselves, though most preferred to remain beautiful. That made it easier to pick them out, but it did nothing to lessen Cat's dread.

She remained in the doorway as a couple walked past her. The man said something to make the woman laugh. Cat's heart caught because she couldn't remember the last time she'd giggled like that —never mind actually being on a date.

Cat squared her shoulders and turned to the left. Her cottage was toward the outskirts of Galway. She couldn't wait to get home where she could relax.

"Relax," she snorted.

There was no such thing for her. While others brushed their cares away with a pint of ale and loud music, she would eat alone at her house and sleep with one eye open.

Being half-Fae had done nothing but make her life miserable.

She'd gotten nothing else from it. Her sister, Nora, had been able to move objects with her mind. Her brother, Domhnall, could grow plants.

For some strange reason, magic had passed her over altogether. No matter how hard she tried, there didn't seem to be a smidgen of magic within her.

Countless times, she'd asked her grandfather what she'd done to not have magic. He'd never quite answered her. In his usual way, he would tell a story about all the Halflings who lived without magic.

But she always suspected that he was keeping something from her.

No amount of conniving or posing the question different ways ever gave her another answer, though. With every year that passed, she was more and more sure that her grandfather was hiding something.

Cat tensed when she walked past a Fae talking to a mortal female. His silver eyes, black hair, and sex appeal were the biggest clues to what he was—Light Fae. At least, it wasn't a Dark.

The Dark scared her the most with their red eyes. She shuddered just thinking about them.

She turned the corner and quickened her pace. Thunder rumbled the same time lightning zigzagged across the sky. More rain was on the way, but if she were lucky, she'd make it back to her cottage before it came.

Suddenly, she stopped. She didn't know what had caught her attention, but something told her to go no farther. Her gaze roamed down the street as people milled about.

There was something in the air that draped over everything like a wet blanket. It took her a moment to realize what it was—

fear. She looked at the humans and saw that none of them appeared to be affected.

Then she heard the footsteps coming, quickly. She saw the man running toward her and looking back over his shoulder. He passed beneath a streetlamp, and she saw his eyes—red.

But it was the terror on his face that surprised her. She hadn't thought there was anything a Dark feared, but whatever was after this particular Fae must be frightening.

Her head told her to run, but her body refused to move. She remained where she was, even as a man appeared out of thin air in front of the Dark.

The Fae slid to a halt, his eyes wide. The man before him had long, white hair that was pulled away from his face by three small braids on each side of his head.

She had little time to process that before she saw the light glint off a blade. The sword sliced through the air and cut down the Dark, turning him to dust in an instant.

Shock reverberated through her as she involuntarily took a step back. What kind of weapon did he have that could kill a Fae?

Because she wanted one.

He took two steps away before he suddenly halted, his body stiffening. Then he gradually turned his head to look right at her. She couldn't make out his face because of the shadows, but she knew he'd seen her.

And then, he disappeared.

She took another step back and hastily looked around, but there was no other sign of the white-haired man. Yet she knew she wasn't alone.

He was there. She was sure of it. Just as she was sure the Fae would come for her soon.

Somehow, she managed to stand her ground. If she were going

to die, she would do it with courage. Even if she was shaking. She wasn't going to run, no matter how much she wanted to.

She felt something behind her a moment before the sound of footsteps reached her. Cat whirled around, ready to face the unknown stranger. But it was a Dark Fae who walked toward her.

"Shite," she murmured and turned back around.

"Hiya, darlin'," the Dark called. "What's your hurry?"

She walked faster and said over her shoulder, "Long day."

"Let me buy you a drink."

"No, thanks."

She waited for him to say more, and when he didn't, she gave a sigh of relief. It wasn't until she was in her cottage that she slumped against the door.

Another day gone.

CHAPTER

two

Fintan stepped in front of the Dark, blocking his advance on the Halfling. "Leave her."

The Dark's red eyes flashed with anger. "I saw her first."

"I'm telling you to leave her. It's your last warning."

The Dark sneered. "Or what?"

"You die."

"Bugger off," he said and tried to push past Fintan.

Fintan called his sword to him. The Dark's eyes widened when he saw it. "I warned you," Fintan said right before he plunged the blade into the Fae's stomach.

At least this time, he was sure no one had seen him. With just a thought, his sword disappeared once more. How had he missed the redhead? He'd never made such a mistake before.

The night had started out good. There was something about hunting that eased his soul. When his quarry was as frightened and impulsive as the Dark Fae he'd been sent to kill, it was even better.

After Death had marked the Darks for dispatch, Fintan had eagerly left Scotland to walk the streets of Ireland once more. Though it had never been his home.

The Fae—both Light and Dark—claimed The Emerald Isle as their own. But for him, the only true home he'd ever known was with the other Reapers.

Fintan veiled himself once more and turned to watch the red-haired Halfling hurry away. Death had set explicit rules for the Reapers, and one was that no Fae could know who they were.

And if someone did see them, they had to die. He'd intended to kill the half-Fae, but when he'd stood behind her, it wasn't alarm or panic he sensed. It had been acceptance.

That single, simple emotion stopped him cold.

He was intrigued, and that surprised him. Perhaps it all came back to what had occurred with Eoghan. For just a second, Fintan allowed his anger to churn in his gut.

There were seven Reapers, but one of them was now gone. They didn't know where Eoghan was or how to find him. No matter how hard they'd searched, there was no sign of their brother.

All because of Bran.

As one of the original Reapers, Bran had broken Death's greatest rule and allowed a Light Fae to know of them, all because he'd been in love with her.

That love had cost the Light her life, which in turn had caused Bran to betray the other Reapers. The only ones who survived were Cael and Eoghan. Cael now led the Reapers.

It was during their last battle with Bran where everything had gone wrong. No matter how Fintan looked at it, he couldn't figure out how they could have stopped what happened.

They didn't know how Bran's magic was continuing to grow, rivaling that of Death's. Despite that, however, they'd nearly won the last battle, ending Bran's revenge once and for all. Help had come from one of the most legendary Light Fae of all time: Rhi.

As they'd battled each other, however, the mix of Bran's and Rhi's magic created a maelstrom, which began ripping the house apart. Bran had used the vortex, directing the energy at Cael, but Eoghan pushed Cael out of the way and was swallowed by the magic instead.

Each of the Reapers was devastated by the loss. More so because Bran had managed to get away in the aftermath.

Fintan hated that Death had wiped Rhi's memories of them. They could really use her help. But it was either erase all mention of the Reapers or kill Rhi.

His thoughts halted when he felt the first drops of rain land on his cheek. Ignoring the coming storm, Fintan found himself following the Halfling. Somehow, she'd escaped Bran's wrath as he and his men systematically hunted and killed every human with Fae blood.

Curious as to how she'd stayed alive, Fintan wanted to know more about her. Too many half-Fae had been wiped out, and he wasn't keen on eliminating another one.

He paused, curious about his thoughts—and feelings. Ever since Eoghan's disappearance, he'd had odd notions. He'd buried all of his feelings long ago, so to have them make themselves known now was disconcerting.

Extremely so.

Fintan continued on. It didn't take him long to find the Halfling. Her stone cottage was quaint. As he walked the perimeter, he was surprised to find that there were no markings used as wards against Fae

There hadn't been shock in her gaze when she'd seen him. That indicated she knew what he was. Which also meant she knew she had Fae blood within her.

Why then didn't she ensure that her home couldn't be invaded?

He stood at the front, looking through the large window. The curtains were drawn, but there was a wide enough slit that he could see her standing in the kitchen, waiting for the kettle to boil. As soon as it did, she poured the water into her cup to make tea.

He watched the way her red hair fell in a thick curtain midway down her back. She moved gracefully as she walked to the sofa and curled up on it. He expected her to turn on the television, as most humans did.

Instead, she picked up a book and began to read. He studied her oval face, noting the delicate shape of her jaw before his gaze moved to her mouth.

Tempting. That's the first thought that came to mind as he looked at her full lips. His gaze moved upward to her cheekbones and her large eyes that were a vivid, emerald green.

The desire swirling within him was like a warning bell going off in his head, demanding he leave. He attempted to squash the feeling, but it was a halfhearted try. The craving, the hunger... felt too damn good.

He couldn't remember the last time he'd experienced any sort of yearning. It kept him rooted to the spot, staring at a woman he could have no part of.

A Reaper pledged himself to Death. There could be no connections to family or friends, no lovers or any sort of relationships outside of the Reapers.

It had been Death's order from the very beginning. It was also something Fintan agreed with completely. A Reaper couldn't do his job if his thoughts were on others.

Yet, Death had altered her rule recently. Baylon had brought Jordyn into their group. Not long after, Kyran brought River, who now carried his child.

The most recent was Neve. She was the newest Reaper and lover to Talin.

Fintan didn't begrudge Jordyn and River being with them. They'd each brought something with them to help hunt Bran, and their being half-Fae was a plus.

But none of that altered his view of a Reaper loving someone. Love could be a dangerous emotion. He should know. He'd exploited it during his reign of terror with ruthless, brutal precision.

He turned when he heard something behind him and found two Light Fae watching the cottage. As the minutes passed, more Fae appeared. Dark and Light stood together, observing the redhead.

Now, more than ever, he wanted to know what it was about the Halfling that drew the interest of others. And if these Fae knew about her, how was it that Bran didn't? Or worse, did Bran know of her and had he allowed her to live?

If that were the case, Fintan needed to know everything there was to know about the woman.

With his decision made, he walked past the Fae and used glamour to change his hair to black and his eyes to silver. Then he dropped the veil and stared at the cottage.

It wasn't long before a female Light Fae stopped beside him. "I've not seen you here before."

He shrugged. "I normally spend my time in Dublin. What's going on?"

"That's Catriona Hayes."

He raised a brow. Obviously, he was supposed to know who this girl was. "Who?"

"Wow," the Light said with a laugh. "You must've been living under a rock. I thought everyone knew who the Hayeses were."

"Tell me," he urged.

She tucked her black hair behind an ear and looked to the cottage as she began. "They've had not one, but three Fae give them children over the last eight hundred years. Of all the Halflings, they are the most powerful."

If that were true, how had he never heard of them before? As of this moment, that would change.

"You watch her. Why?" Fintan asked.

Silver eyes turned to him. "We're waiting for her to die. The rest of her family has been killed. We think it's the Reapers since word has spread that they've returned."

It wasn't as if Fintan could tell her the Reapers had nothing to do with the Halfling deaths. "You think to get a look at a Reaper?"

"No. Well, perhaps," she said with a shrug. "We know her days are numbered, so we watch and wait."

"How ... morbid."

She shrugged indifferently. "It's the way of the mortals. Even ones with magic."

"Why not help her?"

The Light laughed, shaking her head of short, black hair. "Why would we want to do that?"

After the Fae had walked away, Fintan stepped back into the shadows and veiled himself, dropping the glamour at the same time.

The other Reapers would be waiting to hear from him. He should return to their compound on Inchmickery off the coast of

Edinburgh, but he hesitated. In fact, each time he tried to leave, he found that he didn't want to.

Hours passed as Light and Dark came to have a look at Catriona. Even after all the lights were out and the mortal had found her bed for the night, the Fae still milled about in curiosity.

It was an hour before dawn when the last of the Fae left. Fintan had observed it all. Even as the sky began to lighten, he remained. So it was no surprise when he felt a presence near him.

He glanced over and met the dark silver eyes of the leader of the Reapers. "Cael," he said.

One of the gifts granted to them when they'd become Reapers was the ability to remain veiled for as long as they wanted. It also allowed them to see other Reapers when veiled, something no other Fae could do.

Cael came to stand beside him, looking at Catriona's cottage. "Your target was dealt with hours ago."

"I came across something I found curious."

"What's that?"

Fintan made the decision not to tell Cael that Catriona had seen him kill his quarry. He wasn't sure why, but he wanted to keep that to himself. "A Halfling who draws the interest of every Fae in the city. They've watched her house all night."

Cael's brow furrowed as he turned his head to Fintan. "Why?"

"Bran killed her family. They're waiting for her to die, too. And they believe we're responsible for the Halflings' deaths."

"That's not surprising," Cael said, flattening his lips for a moment. "Who is this woman?"

"Catriona Hayes. Apparently, the Fae have visited the family thrice over the years."

"Three times?" Cael asked in shock. "That's unheard of."

Fintan leaned a shoulder against the building he stood near

and crossed his arms over his chest. "She doesn't have marks on the door to keep us out."

"Perhaps she doesn't know what she is."

"She knows."

Thankfully, Cael didn't ask him how he knew such a thing. "Find out what you can. We need to protect her."

Fintan hesitated.

"What is it?" Cael asked.

Fintan blew out a breath. "All of the Fae around here know of Catriona and her family. Doesn't it make sense that Bran would discover that, as well?"

"She should've been his first target," Cael said with distaste. "You think he knows about her and has chosen not to kill her?"

"It's a theory."

"It's a damn good one." Cael blew out a breath. "She could be a pawn to be used for or against Bran."

Fintan wasn't surprised to hear that Cael wanted to use her as bait for Bran. The thought had crossed his mind, as well. He might have suffered the tug of desire, but it would fade soon enough.

Bran was more important.

So was finding Eoghan.

CHAPTER
three

A gnawing, churning sensation that something was about to happen dragged Cat from her slumber. The feeling had been nagging at her ever since she saw the white-haired Fae.

And it continued to intensify.

Throwing off the warmth of her covers, she rose and readied for the day. All the while, her mind kept returning to the Fae and his long, white hair. Her dreams had featured him all night, but she never saw his face.

It was continuously shrouded in shadows.

But he was always watching her.

Living among Fae, she'd learned at an early age to listen to her intuition and give those who made her skin crawl with fear a wide berth. Color her shocked to realize she hadn't felt terror or distress at encountering him.

Her alarm at seeing him had overshadowed that fact until now.

It was enough to put her on edge, which heightened her feeling that something was going to happen.

She finished her tea and rinsed out her mug, setting it on the counter before she grabbed her coat. Her hand was on the doorknob, but she hesitated. There was a part of her brain that urged her to remain inside.

She looked around her home. She'd purposefully left off any protection, so staying inside would do no good. If something were coming for her—and she knew it was—she was determined to face it head-on, not cower in the corner in fear.

No matter the argument her grandfather used, she refused to shield her home. What was the point when she couldn't use the symbols at work since she served both Fae and humans? The Fae could just as easily get to her there or as she walked to and from her home.

Cat yanked open the door and stepped outside. A brisk wind hit her, snatching her breath. She closed the door behind her and started toward the café.

Without meaning to, her gaze locked on the place she'd seen the white-haired Fae. She kept walking, though her mind raced with possibilities of who he might be.

The most plausible answer was that he'd used glamour to change his hair. The Fae's natural hair color was either black or black and silver. Anything else was magic.

That meant he liked to stand out. And he had no problem killing Dark. Which put him in a positive light.

For the moment.

It was his sword she was most interested in. She'd never seen a Fae die. In fact, she hadn't known it was possible to kill one. A blade that could turn them to ash would come in handy to protect her grandfather, as well as herself.

This early in the morning, there were few people on the streets. She liked the solitude. Once inside the café, she began to prep for the day. Before she knew it, her first customer entered.

The hours flew by, giving her little time to think about the white-haired Fae or the anxious feelings inside her. When it was finally time to close, she let out an exhausted sigh. Her feet hurt, and she had the beginnings of a headache.

Yet she hurried home and got into her car, then drove the short distance along the coast to her grandfather's cottage. The white-washed house with its bright red door overlooking the beach always brought back such wonderful memories.

Of a time when there was laughter and love. A time where the future was as bright and beckoning as the sun.

A time when she had been ignorant of the Fae and the part they played in her family.

As she drove over the narrow stone bridge and down the winding drive, some of the fears she carried fell away. No sooner had she put the car in park than her grandfather stepped out of the house with his arms open, a welcoming smile in place.

Cat got out of the vehicle and hurried to him. The feel of his arms around her was comforting. It helped erase the loneliness and gloom of her life. For several minutes, the two remained locked in the embrace.

Then he kissed her forehead. "I missed you, a stóirín, my little darling."

"I missed you, too," she said and looked up at him.

His green eyes were clouded with age, but the love that shone there blazed. His red hair was now completely white, and he had big, bushy eyebrows to complement the wrinkles on his face.

With a wide smile, he said, "Come and tell me how things are."

She was ushered into the small house. When she tried to get

the coffee ready, he tsked and motioned her to a chair. She smiled and sat, basking in her grandfather doting on her. It was a small request that gave him comfort, and one that reminded her of her childhood.

"What do you know of a white-haired Fae?" she asked.

His gaze jerked to her as he set down the mugs on the table. A small frown furrowed his brow. He lowered himself into the chair—slowly because of his age and arthritis—and gave a shake of his head. "You never want to talk of the Fae."

It was true. For years, it was all her siblings had wanted to discuss. Knowing they had magic and she didn't made it difficult for her to want to know about her history with the magical creatures. Yet learn it she had. She'd allowed her siblings to ask the questions, and tucked the answers away.

"Domhnall and Nora did all the talking for me."

He took a sip of coffee heavily laced with sugar. "Did something happen?"

She knew what he was asking. Had someone come after her? So far, she'd been left alone, but that was because she didn't have any magic. To be the only Hayes since the first Halfling not to have any magic was a curse, and yet it was that bane which had kept her alive.

"I saw something last night," she explained. "A Dark was running from this white-haired Fae."

"Everything I know about the Fae states that their hair is either black or black and silver. I've never heard of white. It was probably a glamour."

"He killed a Dark."

Her grandfather's brows shot up on his forehead. "Killed, you say?"

"With a blade that turned the Dark to dust."

Her grandfather sat back in his chair and let out a long sigh. "We might have Fae blood running through our veins, but I've long suspected that we know next to nothing about them. We know the basics, though, which is more than many others can say."

"That weapon could save you."

"Us," her grandfather corrected.

She waved away his words. Without magic, no one cared about her.

Well, that wasn't exactly true. If she had any children, they had the potential to have magic. The thought made her stomach clench in dread. After her childhood, she wouldn't want to put that burden on her children.

But that was something her grandfather didn't need to hear. She took a sip of coffee, then said, "I need to know what kind of blade it was. It might be nothing more than iron. Or a particular metal that we haven't thought of."

"There are tons of legends that say the Fae have an aversion to iron. I can tell you that I've seen a Fae hold a piece of iron, and it did nothing."

Damn. If only it were that easy. She could've picked up a blade from anywhere and used it.

"Did this white-haired Fae speak to you?" her grandfather asked.

"No. He looked my way, but he didn't approach."

Her grandfather's gnarled hand that shook slightly came to rest atop one of hers. "Be careful. You're all I have left, a stóirín."

She saw the sadness in his eyes and decided to change the subject to lighten the mood. She began telling stories of the tourists who came into the café, relaying their antics until he laughed.

The hour lengthened and she cooked, their conversation never ceasing. When they'd finished dinner, her grandfather went to find his pipe while she cleaned off the table and washed the dishes. Cat wiped her hands on the towel when she was done and turned to find her grandfather in the doorway to his study, watching her.

"Stay," he urged.

It was the same argument every time she visited. She couldn't hold his anxious gaze for long. "You know it's better if I don't."

"If they wanted to come for me, they would've already."

"You're safe here."

"I'd feel better if you were with me and not on your own."

She set the towel down and walked to him, taking his hands into hers. "It's only a matter of time before they come for me. If we're not together, they might leave you alone."

"I'd rather die with you than lose the last member of my family."

The sadness in his eyes made her heart clench. "I'm going to find a weapon to use against the Fae, and I'm going to save us both."

"If anyone can, it's you," he replied with a wink and a forced smile.

She hadn't been able to help her parents when they died in a car crash. She hadn't been able to help either of her siblings, but if it was the very last thing she did, Cat would protect her grandfather.

"Is grá liom thú."

"I love you, too," she said and kissed his cheek.

His palm shook as it came to rest against the side of her face. "Perhaps they'll never come for you. Maybe that's why you don't have any magic, a stóirín. Without it, they can't find you."

"Maybe."

As she looked into his eyes that hastily looked away, she knew he was lying. But what about? The Fae coming for her? Or her magic?

It was on the tip of her tongue to ask him, but she knew he wouldn't answer, so she decided against it. They'd had a lovely night, and she didn't want to ruin it by forcing a possible argument. Because once she pushed to know the truth, she wasn't going to relent until she knew all of it.

He walked her to the door where she gave him a hug, squeezing him tightly before walking out of the house. She hated leaving, but she knew he was safer away from her.

"I'll expect you the day after tomorrow," he told her.

She opened her car door and blew him a kiss. "I'll be here."

On the drive home, all the tension that had left while she was at her grandfather's returned with a vengeance, knotting the muscles of her neck and shoulders. She pulled up to her house, the beams from her headlights catching on a figure in the shadows across the street.

With her heart thumping wildly, she put the vehicle in park and got out, facing the road. Her gaze went to where she'd seen the individual. For long moments, nothing moved.

Then, out of the darkness, a shape emerged. He walked slowly toward her wearing a long, black coat that hit him mid-thigh. It wasn't until he stood beneath the streetlight near her drive that she saw his white hair.

Her stomach fell to her feet in dread. Was she now looking into the eyes of her killer? Was he the one who'd slain her brother and sister?

Despite her insides quaking, her intuition wasn't warning her that she should steer clear of him. Stranger still, she didn't fear him—only what he represented. And that was enough to make her look for his sword on his body.

She remained rooted to the spot and lifted her chin, defiance giving her courage. "I won't run."

A white brow quirked as he leaned a hip against the stone wall along the front sidewalk. "Bravery, despite the fear I sense around you."

"Get on with it."

"Just what do you think I've come to do?"

She began to wonder if he intended to play with her before delivering the killing blow. No matter. She still wouldn't show him any fear. "You've come to kill me."

"No."

If only she could see his face instead of having the majority of it hidden by shadows. She wasn't sure if he was joking or not. "What do you want, then?"

A long minute passed while he stood silently. Then he pushed away from the wall and took a step toward her. "To talk."

"If I refuse?" It was better to know how far she could push him from the very beginning.

He shrugged his wide shoulders, the supple leather of his coat moving with him. "Then I leave."

"Just like that?"

"Just like that."

She was curious as to what he wanted, but she wasn't at all sure if talking to him was a good idea. Yet, she was all too aware that he could kill her anytime he wished.

Cat licked her lips, uncertainty giving her pause. Nothing prevented the Fae from entering her house. Nothing would stop him if he wanted to harm her. So why was he asking?

He stood patiently as she debated. Even when a drizzle began, he didn't so much as twitch. She was intrigued by him, so much so that it outweighed everything else. With a nod, she turned and walked to the front door.

Unlocking it, she stepped inside and turned on the lights, wondering if she'd done the right thing. She jumped when the door clicked softly shut behind her. When she whirled around, he stood against the door.

She got her first real look at the Fae. The sight of him left her breathless. It wasn't just his hair that was white, but his eyes, as well. A ring of deep red encircled his iris, making them look unholy. His gaze was intense and penetrating.

Despite the oddity of his coloring, he was mouth-wateringly gorgeous. Though he had an air of despair and sadness about him that made her breath catch.

An angular jaw seemingly cut from stone, and hollowed cheeks gave him a threatening look. Wide, thin lips were flat in his face without any laugh lines, and she wondered if his lips had ever lifted in a smile.

She swallowed as she noted the drops of rain that ran from his coat to drip onto the floor. He kept his gaze on her as he removed the jacket and hung it on a peg.

Her eyes traveled over him, starting with the black button down that clung to his upper body, showing her the thickness of his chest and displaying his muscular arms. Unable to help herself, she let her eyes move lower to his trim hips and long legs encased in black denim.

She became aware of the very masculine, very gorgeous specimen who now stood in her home. When she glanced up, his gaze snagged hers. She wasn't able to look away, and she found she didn't want to.

They stared at each other wordlessly. She knew she should be afraid of him, but for some odd reason, she wasn't. No matter how she searched for an explanation, she couldn't figure out why. Her misplaced trust might be her downfall in the end.

"Who are you?" she asked.

His shoulders lifted as he took in a breath. "Fintan."

"Fintan," she repeated. "I'm—"

"Catriona," he interrupted her.

So he knew of her. Of course, he did. She looked down to find her purse still gripped tightly in her fingers. She set it down and shrugged out of her coat, lying it across a chair. Then she turned back to him. "I've never seen a Fae like you."

"Because there is no other like me."

She suspected no truer words had ever been spoken.

CHAPTER

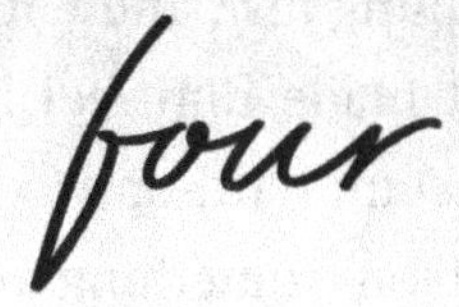

Being this near to Catriona put Fintan in an awkward predicament because he wanted to be closer.

He craved it, longed for it.

Yearned for it.

The same lust he'd felt the night before made his blood run hot and caused desire to pound through him now. It blindsided him, consuming him until all he could think about was pulling her against him and tasting her lips.

What was fekking wrong with him?

He didn't desire or long for anything other than the justice he served for Death. And yet, here he was.

Aching.

With every beat of his heart that demanded he go to her, his iron will kept him embedded in place. He was rational, calm, and cool in all things.

The rash, reckless thoughts now running through his mind

were far from normal. In fact, they frightened him a little because of how fiercely he wanted to give in.

He'd gone thousands of years without feeling even a tiny nugget of anything resembling lust, and with one look at Catriona, he'd been bowled over. It made him feel like a randy teen, who walked around with a constant hard-on.

He focused his mind on something other than tearing her clothes off. Her green eyes watched him as a fox might watch a hound. No longer did he sense fear, but she wasn't exactly comfortable with his presence either.

Not that he could blame her. No one was ever comfortable around him. He could ease everyone by using glamour, but to be honest, he didn't give a fuck. This was who he was. Either they got used to him, or they didn't. It didn't matter to him.

Or it usually didn't.

"You're Dark."

He didn't pretend her words were a question. "Aye."

"If you're not here to kill me, then why did you want to speak with me?"

A good question. He'd followed her to her grandfather's and watched their interaction. He hadn't been allowed inside because of the carved symbols around the doorways. But he'd seen enough to know that Cat and her grandfather were close.

He hadn't intended to show himself to her that night. He could've remained veiled, but he'd let it drop—he'd let her see him. There was something about her that enticed him.

Was it her bravery or her beauty?

He'd meant to formulate a plan and use glamour to disguise himself to get close to her so he could be prepared when Bran showed up. That plan was forgotten when he saw her step out of her car and look his way.

"Fintan?"

What had she asked? Oh, that's right. "I want to know about you."

"What for?" she asked with a bemused expression.

"It's not as common as you might think for a Fae to leave a human with a child. It's even rarer for three of my kind to visit the same family."

She blew out a harsh breath and turned her back to him, her head bowed as she put her hands on the back of a kitchen chair. "So I'm a curiosity you've come to study?"

"I want to know what it is about your family that continues to draw the Fae."

Her head lifted. "I don't have magic. It doesn't seem to matter how many Fae decide to screw someone in my family, not everyone gets something."

He could argue with her, but Fintan decided it was best to let her think what she would. Her words were clipped, angry. That kind of resentment could only be the result of something as horrid as a death. Then he recalled what the Light Fae the previous night had told him about Catriona's family being killed.

Yet not everyone in her family was dead.

"Who did you lose?"

"My brother and sister." She turned to face him then.

Fintan fisted his hands so he wouldn't reach for her when he spotted the raw, visceral pain in her eyes. He was a Reaper, and that meant he lived alone. There could be no feelings of desire or longing.

With a savage shove, he tamped down such emotions.

"Why didn't they come for me?" she demanded with her eyes ablaze with rage and grief.

"I don't know." It was one of the reasons he was interested in her.

She snorted and walked into the kitchen. There, she grabbed a bottle of red wine and took out a glass. She held it up, silently asking him if he wanted any. Fintan gave a shake of his head and watched as she poured the liquid.

She took a drink and stared into the glass. "My grandfather thinks it's because I don't have any magic, but I know he's wrong. The Reapers are toying with me."

He jerked at the mention of Reapers. So she, like the other Fae, assumed his group was responsible for the deaths. "What do you know of the Reapers?"

"I hear things. Some Fae might attempt to hide what they are, but none of them try to keep their conversations secret. I suspect it's because they believe mortals are beneath them. What do you know about the Reapers?"

"Why are you so sure it's them after you?"

Her head jerked up as her gaze clashed with his. "Possibly because my family has lived in this town among the Fae for eight hundred years without any Hayeses being murdered."

"There was a mass killing of Halflings around the world," Fintan said after a minute. "I heard a rumor that it's the Reapers who stopped the murders."

Green eyes narrowed a fraction. "Then who began it?"

"A group who wanted to make it look as if the Reapers were responsible."

She took a drink, seeming to considering his words. "I don't suppose it matters what group killed my siblings. In the end, it was a Fae."

"Would you feel the same had it been a human?"

"That's different."

He raised a brow. "It isn't. You're part of both worlds."

She swallowed and lowered her gaze. "I'll reluctantly admit that I hadn't thought of it that way."

He found his lips softening as if attempting to smile—something he halted instantly. "I know what's coming for you."

"How?"

"Does it really matter?" he asked.

"No, I suppose not. Why would you tell me?"

"I want to kill him."

She walked to the sofa and sat. Then she motioned to the loveseat, indicating that he should sit. "Him. So it's one man?"

"I want to kill the leader of a particular group of Fae."

"Why?"

He walked to the loveseat but remained standing. "Revenge."

"So you want to use me as bait to catch him."

"I do." Fintan sat on the edge of the chair. "Help me get vengeance for your family and the other humans who died because they had Fae blood."

"Your offer is ... appealing."

"Except?"

"I have nothing with which to protect myself."

He found he liked her more and more. She didn't ask for him to protect her, but a way to defend herself. Her fearlessness only made his lust grow. "I'll be with you."

"No."

"Fae stand outside your house during the night, waiting for the day when Bran comes for you."

That news didn't seem to faze her. She drank more of the wine and crossed one leg over the other. "I want a weapon like yours. The one that can turn a Fae to dust."

"I can make that happen, but I'll still be with you."

"I can't have a Fae with me all the time. It'll draw attention."

He didn't remind her that she was the one who drew attention. Whether she knew it or not, he was going to be with her. There was no way he'd leave her alone for even one moment.

Because catching Bran meant they could find Eoghan. After that, Fintan would take great pleasure in killing Bran slowly for all that he'd done.

A lock of red hair fell into Catriona's eyes. She moved it aside, her gaze on him. "And when you catch this Fae? Will I be left alone?"

"If that is your wish."

"You'll give me such a promise?"

He gave a nod.

"Who are you to be able to do such a thing?"

"Does it matter?"

Her eyes widened as if alarmed by his words. "Yes."

"I give you my word."

She set her wine on the table next to her. "I don't know you. You may be very honorable. I'm counting on that as we work together because we have a mutual enemy. But, let's be honest. Once we've apprehended your prey, you'll leave. You won't have any idea what happens to me. Nor do I expect you to. What I want is your promise that you and those connected to me won't kill me or my family."

"They won't. I give you my vow."

They both knew she had no choice but to accept his promise. It was the first time his word had been questioned, and he didn't like it. Never mind that he knew she had valid arguments.

All of this was based on the idea that Bran would kill her, but Fintan was keeping his options open in case things went the other way. The Hayeses being the most powerful Halfling family wasn't something a power-hungry Bran would allow to slip through his fingers. Which meant Bran didn't know about Cat.

Yet.

"Then we have a deal," she said and held out her hand.

He looked at it, both eager to touch her and realizing it wouldn't be a good idea. Still, he reached out and clasped her hand.

With a firm shake, she released him. All the while, his skin tingled where their palms had met. The desire he thought he'd rid himself of returned with a vengeance—and a hunger that threatened to break apart his icy restraint.

His gaze lowered to her lips. He saw them moving as she spoke, but all he could think about was kissing her. It took a full minute before he was able to get himself back under control.

"We can work out the details later," she said.

Fintan mentally shook himself to clear his head. "There will be few details. I'll make sure our enemy knows you're here. Then we wait for him to appear."

"This Fae's name is Bran?"

He glanced at her lips again. "Aye."

"What makes you think he'll come?"

"He wants to rid this realm of every Halfling."

"And the Reapers?"

He stood. "What of them?"

"What if they show up?"

"They won't."

She rolled her eyes. "How can you be sure?"

"I'm sure they have other things to do."

"Right." Catriona got to her feet. "I want this to be over. I want my grandfather to be able to leave his house again. I want to stop looking over my shoulder."

That caused him to raise a brow. "Will you?"

"What?"

"Stop looking over your shoulder once Bran is caught?"

She shrugged, her lips twisting. "I'd like to think I will. By the way, how do you know the Fae responsible is named Bran?"

"It's a long story."

"I like long stories."

Once more, he found himself wanting to grin. "He's an old enemy who likes to cause trouble. I'm the kind of Fae who likes to make such men go away."

"That wasn't such a long story."

"It's the condensed version."

To his surprise, her lips tilted in a soft smile. "When do we start?"

"We already have. Sleep easy tonight, Catriona. I'll be watching over you."

Fintan grabbed his coat and started for the door.

"Cat."

He paused and looked at her over his shoulder. "What?"

"Call me Cat. Everyone does."

He gave a nod and walked from the house. As soon as he was outside and the other Fae saw him, they scattered. In the next step, he veiled himself. No one, especially other Fae, needed to see what he was about.

Cat surprised him. He'd expected some sort of resistance about being bait, but then he hadn't counted on her courage or willingness to stand and fight.

There was fire inside her, a need to live that overrode her fear. That could be a deciding factor if Bran did come for her—but not to kill her.

If Cat had even a bit of magic, she could protect herself. The fact that she had none left her exposed. And it made him wonder how, in a family as powerful as hers, she didn't have magic.

He thought of the weapon she'd asked for. The Fae weren't in the habit of giving Halflings things that could kill the Fae, but in this case, she was justified in asking. And he was going to make sure she got her weapon.

Once in the shadows across the street, he turned toward the cottage. His gaze locked on the front window where Cat stood, staring outside. Her eyes wandered around. Was she looking for him?

He hoped so. Then he instantly regretted his thoughts. It was Eoghan's sacrifice and disappearance that had upset the balance of things. It had to be that, which was causing him to ... feel.

Or was it?

Fintan drank in the sight of Cat's face before she snapped the curtains closed.

CHAPTER
five

Death's Realm

For thousands of years, Cael's course had been laid before him. He'd carried out Death's orders, knowing he was helping to keep the balance.

From the first moment he'd accepted the position, he'd felt as if he had a mission. As if he finally belonged.

That feeling hadn't changed, only solidified. He'd been born to be a Reaper, to be Death's executioner. It was a role that had some benefits, but many detriments. Though few of those disadvantages bothered him.

He had everything he'd ever needed in his men.

Quickly, he halted the next thought that began the moment he thought of Death as he walked through the Fae doorway that only the two of them could see.

He blew out a breath. So much had changed for the Reapers in a very short time, and he wasn't sure what the future held.

Regardless, he knew his role. He would stand with Death until the end of time.

Pushing such thoughts aside, he looked around at the thick foliage of Death's realm. Trees stretching high into the sky swayed with the gentle wind. He followed a path that meandered through the various plants and flowers that grew in dense clusters.

Bees buzzed while the songs of dozens of birds rang through the air. A dragonfly darted in front of him before zipping around and flying higher.

Cael's gaze landed on the white tower that rose before him, gleaming in the sunlight. Every time he came to this realm, he was reminded of all that he'd worked for.

It still boggled his mind that he'd come from being the last of the first seven Reapers to the leader of a new group. He and Eoghan had survived Bran's betrayal only to learn that Bran had escaped the Netherworld and set a course for retaliation.

It had begun with the slaughter of millions of Halflings. Now, Eoghan was ... gone. Cael refused to believe that his friend was dead. It was why he'd begun to search different realms, in the hopes of finding some clue.

So far, there had been nothing.

"Your worries weigh heavily upon your shoulders," said a soft, feminine voice behind him.

He closed his eyes for a moment, savoring the sound of her words before he turned to face Death. He gazed into her fathomless, lavender eyes and was lost.

In her beautiful gaze, he felt as insignificant as a speck of dirt in the cosmos. Because she alone had endured from the beginning of time, standing in judgment of those who disrupted the balance.

Exquisite didn't begin to describe her. She was timeless and ethereal. She had a face so perfect that she put every Fae to shame.

Impossibly high cheekbones and a mouth that he hungered to taste only added to her allure.

"Yes," he replied as he looked at her wealth of black hair piled atop her head while wisps of ebony curls fell about her face and neck artfully.

It drew his gaze to her creamy, unblemished skin. She wore her favorite attire – a black gown with a long, full skirt.

The satin molded her to her upper body, accentuating her small waist and the curvature of her breasts. The neck rounded slightly as it came all the way up to her collarbones. The sleeves were of the same satin and stopped at her wrists. The satin skirt had nary a wrinkle or crease. Every edge was trimmed with a bright green thread in a Celtic design.

"Mine, as well," she said and turned away.

His eyes locked on the deep V of the back of the dress that dropped to her waist. He longed to run his fingers down her spine, but he held himself in check.

No one touched Death.

"Why did you come?" Erith asked.

He followed her, watching as butterflies trailed behind her. Even the flowers seemed to turn toward her as she neared them. He was forever awed watching her.

"It's Fintan," he said.

She glanced over her shoulder. "He carried out my judgment on the Dark as effortlessly as always. Was there a problem?"

"There never is with him."

"My cold Reaper. You worry because he hides his emotions."

"He doesn't hide them. Fintan no longer has them."

Erith stopped and turned slightly to look at him, a black brow raised. "His feelings are still there. Fintan had reason to bury them. It was the best thing for him."

Each of the Reapers had experienced a betrayal that led to their deaths. It was how Erith had chosen them. Once in the group, it was up to each Reaper if they wanted to share their story. Fintan had never spoken of his past.

Death, however, had given Cael the story to each of the Reapers so he could better lead them. He never let any of them know because sometimes pasts were better left forgotten.

"While Fintan hunted the Dark, he came across a Halfling," Cael told her.

Erith continued walking toward the tower. "I assume he believes Bran will come for this Halfling."

"It's a possibility."

"Or?" she prompted, glancing at him over her shoulder.

Cael watched a curl bounce alongside her neck. "There's the possibility Bran might want her."

"Which is why he hasn't killed her," Erith said with a nod.

"Either way, Fintan wants to set a trap using the Halfling."

Death was quiet until they reached the tower. There was a curse that drifted down from one of the windows. She smiled sadly. "Seamus is still searching for how Bran is giving his army so much power."

Cael didn't bother to mention that he knew Seamus also searched for how her magic seemed to be diminishing. There was a connection between her and Bran that allowed the ex-Reaper to grow stronger as Death weakened.

It was one of the many reasons Cael wanted to kill Bran.

"Tell me of this Halfling," Erith urged as she moved to a table and chairs and sat.

Cael followed her, sitting across from her. "I was hoping you might know her."

"The name?"

"Catriona Hayes."

Death sat back. "I've not thought about the Hayes family in decades. Three Fae visited the family, each leaving a child."

"So Fintan was told by a Light in Galway. Why did the Fae continue to go to the family?"

"At one time, the Hayeses were powerful, ruling Galway. I believe that, combined with a comely female, caught the attention of the first Light. It's probably what caused all three of the Fae to spend time with them."

"It's very rare for that to happen."

"It also means the family has more magic than any other half-Fae. They could rival the Druids," she added.

He ran a hand over his chin. "Why would Bran not go after the family first?"

"Who's to say he didn't? Maybe one of the family kept under the radar. She would be a perfect lure to draw him out if she's willing to go along with the plan."

"She's not hiding."

Death drummed her fingers slowly on the table. "Now I know why you think Bran might want her."

Cael leaned forward, bracing his forearms on his knees. "I'm not sure Fintan is the right one to talk to her."

"Because he hides his emotions or because of his looks?"

"Both. You know how he unsettles even the Dark."

Erith regarded him in silence for a moment. "Fintan is too smart to let this opportunity slip past us. He—like all of us—has a driving need to find Eoghan."

At the mention of his oldest friend, Cael rose to his feet and faced the thick forest. "Eoghan saved my life. I won't ever stop looking for him."

"Nor will I."

He looked down to find Death beside him. A fire burned in her lavender eyes, one that promised retribution against Bran. He had the urge to touch her face, to have some sort of connection with her.

"We will find Eoghan," she promised.

"Bran will never tell us."

Her chin lifted defiantly. "I'm Death. I will find my Reaper."

If there was one thing he knew about Erith, it was that she was always true to her word. Though she looked the same, he could sense that she wasn't well.

Every day that passed and more of her magic was syphoned, the weaker she became. The world would be flung into chaos with Death's demise—if it came to that.

And he ... he wasn't sure he could survive not having her near.

"And if Bran finds you?"

Her eyes flashed dangerously. "Do you forget who I am?"

"Never."

"But?" she asked, her gaze narrowing.

With just a thought, she could cease his life. The power within her didn't inspire fear. He respected and admired her. But she didn't frighten him.

Some might call that foolish since she was Death, but few knew her. Not that he claimed to know her. But he was closer than most.

It was because of that, that he knew how deeply she cared for the Reapers. He alone had seen the extremes she had gone to for them. He alone knew how much she wanted them to be happy and find the peace that had eluded them in life.

"You trust me enough to lead your men."

"Your Reapers," she corrected.

He shook his head. "You chose us. We're yours."

There was some unnamed emotion that flashed in her eyes, but it was gone in a blink. "If I didn't trust you, you wouldn't be leading them."

"Yet you don't trust me enough to tell me that your magic is fading."

Her gaze slid away. A wall came down between them in a heartbeat. She became as aloof as she'd once been. It cut him deeper than any blade could.

He knew it was wrong to desire her. He knew it was wrong to want more than he could have with her, but he couldn't stop what had been set in motion.

Everyone who saw her wanted Erith. He'd thought himself above the others because he was her chosen leader, the one she allowed into her realm. But he'd been wrong.

That was never clearer than at that moment.

He took a deep breath and released it. "I'll keep you updated on Fintan's progress. If this Hayes woman is as special as you say, that should pull Bran out of his hiding place."

Minutes passed as he waited for Death to reply. Finally, he realized she wasn't going to. He bowed his head and pivoted to make his way back to the Fae doorway.

With every step away from her, his gut clenched. She was Bran's ultimate target. Her realm had always kept her safe from anyone she didn't allow in, but how long would that last now?

If her magic had faded enough to let the sole doorway into the Netherworld prison where Bran had been kept become visible, allowing Seamus to find it and help Bran escape, then it was simply a matter of time before Bran found his way to her realm.

Since there was only one doorway to her, Cael intended to guard it until Bran was captured. The only way Bran would ever get to Erith was if he killed Cael first.

It didn't matter that she didn't feel anything for him. It didn't even matter that she was more than capable of taking care of herself. If Cael could do this for her, then he would.

Because of who she was.

Because his feelings were forbidden.

Because there could never be anything more than what he saw in his dreams.

He walked through the doorway, stopping himself from looking back at the last minute. There, on a small isle in the middle of a loch in Scotland, he set up sentry.

CHAPTER
six

The silence of the night could be disconcerting to some, but Cat always found it a time for reflection, when no outside noises could interfere. And she had much to think about.

She'd lain awake in her bed, staring at the ceiling while she came at Fintan's proposition from every angle. She was taking a chance trusting him, but what did she have to lose, really? Already, she felt as if each day were borrowed time. Why not make use of it while she could?

To take a stand—in any way possible.

Her thoughts drifted to Fintan. His voice was deep and so captivating that she wondered if he used it on purpose. Almost like a weapon, but one of silk and seduction instead of steel and blood.

He made her nervous, but she also wanted to know more about him. Particularly how he'd come to have white hair. But also, she was curious about everything he kept tightly locked away. She recognized it in him because she did it herself.

Though he was a master while she was only a novice.

Fintan had been upfront with her with everything, which she appreciated. He hadn't pulled any punches, telling her about Bran and that he would come for her. It was everything she already knew, but he hadn't tried to soften things.

Her predicament turned her thoughts to her grandfather. He was the last family she had, and she was willing to do whatever it took to keep him unharmed. She was young and able to continue the Hayes lines. With her gone, there was a chance Bran and the Fae would leave her grandfather alone. It was a gamble she was counting on.

Thinking of family soon had memories of her siblings and parents running through her head, causing her to smile, laugh, and even cry.

She didn't push those thoughts away. They were the only way her family lived on, and she would welcome the happiness—and the pain—the memories brought.

Before she knew it, light filtered through her curtains, signaling the start of a new day. It was her day off, but habit got her up at the normal time. She showered and dressed, wondering how the day would unfold.

When she opened her front window curtains, she expected to see Fintan. When she didn't, she shrugged. That's what she deserved for believing he'd watch over her the entire night.

She turned and then jumped back at the sight of Fintan sitting at her kitchen table.

"My apologies," he said. "I didn't want anyone to see me enter."

His voice caused warmth to spread over her like a seductive

whisper. Or maybe it was the way those red-rimmed white eyes watched her as if she were his next meal—in bed.

Either way, how her body heated in response caused her to take a step toward him as if some invisible string were tugging her forward.

"How long have you been there?" she asked.

"I just popped in."

She swallowed and made her way to the kitchen on unsteady legs to put bread in the toaster. "I suppose you're here for the details." When he didn't reply, she looked over her shoulder at him.

He slowly nodded his head once.

"All right. Where do we begin?" she asked as she spread butter on her toast.

"Some friends of mine are spreading the word about you."

She narrowed her gaze at him. "I suspect there's a but in there somewhere."

"With the amount of Fae that know about you, I find it ... strange that Bran doesn't."

A chill raced down her spine, halting her movements. "In other words, he could've been watching me all along?"

"Yes."

She set down the toast, her appetite now gone. Turning to him, she said, "I hope I'm doing the right thing."

"It's too late to change your mind."

"I'm not. I'm trusting you, and—"

"You don't trust Fae," he finished.

She gave a shake of her head. "I've had no reason to."

"Until recently, you didn't have a reason to distrust us either."

"Do you have any idea how hard it is to be a part of two worlds, but not belong to either one?"

"Yes," he stated softly.

As she looked at his white hair and eyes, she realized he did indeed know how she felt. She walked to the table and sat. "So, what happens now?"

"We wait." Then he placed something on the table.

Cat gaped in astonishment and excitement when she saw the dagger. It was longer than a normal blade with a white wooden handle polished to a shine. Thin strips of gold made a design of swirls around the grip that was anything but feminine.

She eagerly picked up the weapon and slid it from the sheath. The weight was surprisingly light, balancing well in her hand. The blade was slightly curved with both edges sharpened.

"It was forged in the Fires of Erwar," he said. "It'll slay any Fae."

"Fires of Erwar?"

"A mountain on the Fae realm where the fires are mixed with magic. Any blade forged there will scar or kill a Fae."

She looked into his eyes and smiled. He could have no idea what the weapon meant to her. But it was enough that he had granted her request. "Thank you."

"Are you skilled with such a weapon?"

Cat shrugged. "No."

"I suspected as much."

"Then why did you give it to me?" she asked, confused.

He tilted his head slightly. "Because Bran will come with several men and they won't expect you to have it. It'll give you some time."

"For?" she asked.

"For me to reach you."

She put the dagger into the sheath and set it back on the table, her excitement dulled a little. "I know there's a chance Bran will kill me."

"I don't intend to allow that to happen."

"Be that as it may, you can't watch over me twenty-four hours a day. I want you to know that I'm not going into this blindly. I know my chances."

He blinked. "Your odds improved with my arrival."

She couldn't help but laugh at his comment. "I think you're right, even if I don't know you."

"I don't know you either."

"You know more about me than I do you."

"What do you want to know?" he asked.

She opened her mouth to pose her first question when her mobile phone rang. She answered it, frowning as she tried to make sense of the mass of jumbled words the caller kept repeating. Then she heard it.

"The café is on fire!"

Cat dropped the phone and rushed from the house, her arms pumping as she ran to the café. Something stopped her from entering the building that was now engulfed by bright red flames. She looked down at the thick arms banding her middle and recognized Fintan.

"It's too late," he whispered in her ear.

She had no choice but to watch as a team of men fought the fire to no avail. All around her, people milled about, bumping into her, but she didn't pay them any mind.

The café that had been in her family for over a hundred years was no more. Something else had been taken from her. It felt as if someone were intentionally attacking her, taking away things that meant the most to her.

"Cat," Fintan said.

She let him lead her away. As they turned back toward her house, she glanced his way to see that he'd used glamour to hide his appearance.

But it was the way his gaze darted about that put her on edge.

"What is it?" she asked.

"Magic started that fire."

She shook her head in bewilderment. "Why? I serve the Fae as well as humans. All are welcome."

"Then it's probably Bran."

It was said with such certainty that she frowned. "What does burning down the source of my income get him?"

Fintan's eyes met hers. "I don't know. It could be a test to draw me out."

"Did you see him?"

"No, but that doesn't mean anything. He can stay veiled for as long as he wants."

She stumbled to a halt, shock making her blood run cold. "What? That's the kind of information I could use."

"Now you know."

Cat rolled her eyes. "Just like a male."

She started walking. There was insurance on the café. That would help her get back on her feet. It would take months, though.

"I'm going to have to tell my grandfather." That wouldn't be easy.

Fintan looked over his shoulder. "At least he's well guarded. Tell me why you don't have the same symbols on your house."

"Did you follow me to my grandfather's house?"

"Yes."

No excuses, just a simple answer. And she was coming to like the way he stated such things. "I want the Fae to leave him alone.

He's an old man who has lost everything. He shouldn't have to suffer any more."

"He'll suffer if you die."

She shot Fintan a look. "I know."

"He thinks you have the same wards up?" he guessed.

Reluctantly, she nodded. "I lied because I know he's an easy target. I want them to come for me first."

"You're going to get your wish."

That she was. "It's not like I want to die."

"You could've fooled me."

She took offense at his words. "It's inevitable."

"Death for mortals is certain, but openly inviting death into your home is tantamount to madness."

Her mouth fell open, but he continued before she had a chance to speak.

"You say your grandfather has lost everyone. He still has you. How much longer do you think he'd have the will to live once you were killed?"

"I can bear children. I can continue the line. If someone wants to wipe out our family, they'll come for me first."

Fintan stopped and faced her as they reached her cottage. "So you serve yourself up for sacrifice?"

"To give my grandfather a chance. Yes."

Fintan was quiet for a long time as he stared at her. "I'd do the same for the men I call my brothers."

His words touched her, and she put her hand on his arm without thinking. His eyes jerked down to where she touched his jacket. Yanking her hand away, she turned and walked down the sidewalk to the front door.

When she entered, Fintan was already inside with the glamour removed. His revelation about his brothers made him seem more human. She knew Fae had emotions, but there was something about him that made her think of him as a robot most times.

She'd seen him kill, so she knew he was skilled with his sword. It had been in the way he moved and the way he held the weapon.

But he had yet to smile. The only thing that came close to any emotion was the few times she'd seen him frown.

That was until she'd heard him talk about his brothers. Under it all, she perceived fierce protection and loyalty in his voice. He cared about those men. Deeply.

"I loved my brother and sister," she said as she made coffee. "And they loved me. It wasn't anyone's fault that I was born without magic. While they honed their skills and learned to control their gifts, I was relegated to watching them. I was an outsider, unable to be a part of what they enjoyed."

"That must've been tough."

"My parents constantly told me that I would come into my gifts one day. I believed them until I turned twenty. When that day came and went, I knew that, for whatever reason, the magic had passed me over."

Fintan came to stand near her. "Has that happened to anyone else in the Hayes line?"

"Never."

He put his finger beneath her chin and turned her head to him. "You're far from being the only Halfling without magic. Many of the half-Fae have none. So don't let that diminish who you are."

Heat started from the point of contact of his finger and spread over her body. He spoke with conviction, that sexy voice adding a layer that made her heart skip a beat.

Her mouth went dry when his gaze lowered to her lips. She wasn't sure if she wanted him to kiss her or not. The longer they remained locked in place, the more she yearned for him to do something.

She found herself leaning toward him bit by bit. Something swirled inside her, and it took a moment for her to realize what it was—longing.

Suddenly, he dropped his hand and took a step back. "The coffee has finished brewing."

"Yeah." She turned to the machine.

While she'd been wrapped in desire, he'd been listening to the pot brew. She was such an idiot. Was she so lonely that she was ready to fall for the first man who gave her a second look?

Apparently.

She poured two mugs and took hers to the sofa. The day had barely begun, and already, she'd lost the source of her income, been overcome by desire, and faced more truths than she could process.

At least she hadn't tried to kiss Fintan. What a fool she'd have made of herself.

CHAPTER

seven

Desire, as hot as lava, burned through Fintan. It was all he could do to not let loose the raging hunger that demanded a taste of Cat.

Touching her had been his biggest mistake of the last millennium. His body roared with a hunger so great that his knees threatened to buckle.

Then he'd looked into her emerald eyes. Passion shone as bright as the sun. Time stopped, as if the connection of their bodies had been the trigger.

He'd been unable to look away, powerless to think of anything other than her.

As she'd leaned toward him, he'd inwardly smiled. Despite his coloring, she wanted him, desired him. His emotions swelled and burst through his carefully constructed wall. He was drowning in them, but she was his anchor.

She stood as steady as an oak while she beckoned him with her guileless gaze. In all his eons of time, he couldn't remember wanting anything as much as he did her in that moment.

He forgot Bran, forgot he was a Reaper. The world and everyone in it simply vanished as if it had never existed.

Then a lock of her hair fell against the back of his hand. He looked at the deep red strands, a bellow rising within him as the link between them was severed.

His vows to Death and the Reapers replayed in his mind, reminding him of his responsibilities. And they didn't include making love to a Halfling.

Fintan dropped his arm and moved away from her. He fisted his hand as his fingers pulsed from his contact with Cat. Another roar filled him, this one for what could've been.

He swallowed past the lump of regret. Movement out of the corner of his eye had his head turning to the window. He jerked as he recognized Searlas, Bran's lieutenant.

With Cat shouting his name, Fintan rushed out of the house after Searlas. No sooner was Fintan outside, than the Dark smiled and vanished.

"Who was that?" Cat asked as she came to stand behind Fintan, breathing heavily.

"Searlas. He's one of Bran's men."

"So it worked."

"Aye." He turned in a circle to make sure Searlas had left the area. Then found himself caught by Cat's gaze.

A small frown puckered her brow. Then she looked over his shoulder, her lips parting as her eyes grew round. He turned and saw the black smoke rising in the distance.

"No," she whispered and ran to her car.

She fumbled with the door, and then slammed her hands

against the vehicle when it wouldn't open. "No," she said again and dashed around the car toward the house.

Fintan teleported in front of her. He grabbed her arms to halt her and made her look at him. "Forget the keys."

"It's my grandfather," she said and tried to shove him away.

He knew exactly where the fire was coming from. Without another word, he teleported them to the seaside cottage. The house remained intact and unscathed.

It was the small shed behind it that burned, causing the smoke to rise thick and black toward the heavens. In a blink, Cat was out of his arms, running to the house as she called for her grandfather.

Fintan didn't follow. The wards on the house would prevent a Fae from entering, but with Bran's power, he could've set the cottage on fire. Why hadn't he?

Fintan's gaze turned to the shed as a sinking feeling came over him. While Cat continued to shout for her grandfather as she searched the cottage, Fintan made his way to the outbuilding.

He spotted the smoking, charred body and briefly closed his eyes. The fire roared out of control, consuming the shed and everything around it.

It was easy enough to put out the fire with magic. He was debating what to do with the body and how to tell Cat when he turned around.

His gaze immediately landed on her. She stood a few feet from him, staring at the body of her grandfather. Her face was ashen, her eyes glazed.

There was no doubt in his mind that Searlas started the fire at the café. But why? And why kill the old man? To hurt Cat? Or to prove that they were in control?

Fintan thought it might be the latter. That meant Bran knew it was a trap. And it confirmed that Bran had known about Cat all along.

As Fintan stared at Cat, he watched as the shock of the scene settled over her. After a moment, she turned and walked away. He looked at the dead man before he set up wards around the area that would alert him if anyone—human or Fae—broke the barrier.

When he finally finished, he went looking for Cat. He found her sitting on the beach, watching the waves roll in. Unsure if Bran or his men were near and veiled, Fintan pushed out with his magic but felt nothing.

"For now," he whispered.

He made his way to Cat and sank onto the sand beside her. She looked lost, forlorn. And it did something to him. Some nameless emotion sparked within him.

Then he recognized it for what it was: wrath. For all that Cat had lost, for everything that she had endured simply because she was a Halfling.

"He was all I had," she said. "And he died alone."

Her head turned to Fintan. As he watched, her eyes welled up with tears, and the moisture spilled down her cheeks in a flood.

"I should've been here," she cried before burying her head in her hands.

Fintan wasn't good with tears. In fact, he didn't know what to do. He lifted a palm to place it on her back but stopped just short of touching her. Fisting his hand, he lowered it to the sand.

Her shoulders shook with grief, and for the first time in his life, he felt helpless. Something in the back of his mind urged him to give her some kind of comfort.

Gritting his teeth, he scooted closer. It took him two tries before he was able to lift his arm. He kept it hovering over her shoulders, unsure if it was the right thing to do.

But her pain sliced through him as easily as a hot knife through butter.

He lowered his arm, draping it across her back. When she didn't shove him away, he tightened his grip. Her heart-wrenching tears continued. Then, to his surprise, she rested her head on his shoulder.

It was the first time in his very long life anyone had turned to him for solace. He knew he was doing it all wrong, but he couldn't imagine being anywhere else.

The longer she lingered, the more at ease he became in this new role. There was no need for words. There was nothing he could say that would lessen her anguish.

Finally, her tears began to lessen. To his surprise—and joy— she remained in her position. He looked down to see her wet lashes spiked, and tear streaks down her face.

But he also saw courage. Though he suspected he was just now seeing the real Cat. The world had beaten her down, taking every-thing from her little by little.

Yet she endured. She might stumble, but she didn't stop. She put everyone else before herself. She didn't fight what she thought was her fate. Instead, she worked it to her advantage.

It took a special kind of woman to do that.

"Tell me about Bran," she urged. "My grandfather always told me that in order to prevail, I must know my enemy completely."

Fintan blew out a breath. If anyone deserved the story of Bran, it was Cat. Unfortunately, that meant he had to tell her who he was.

Death's rules echoed in his mind. He would be betraying one of his vows by telling Cat. That didn't sit well with him, but Bran's rampage wouldn't stop anytime soon.

So, with a deep breath, he made his decision.

"What do you know of the Reapers?" Fintan asked.

She drew in a deep breath. "They're legends. Stories, really, to frighten Fae children. At least that's what I always thought until I began to hear the Fae around town speak of them as if they were real."

"The Reapers are real. Bran was one."

"Was?" she asked and sat up to look at him. "What happened?"

Fintan looked out at the water. "Perhaps you should know that if I tell you what you ask, Death could kill you."

"Death? As in a person?"

"Yes. It's forbidden for the Fae to know anything about the Reapers."

There was a slight pause before she said, "You're Fae."

He glanced at her but didn't answer.

"I'm a Halfling," she said. "Does that matter?"

"No," he replied. "It doesn't."

She licked her lips. "I've got Bran after me. I need to know."

"Death is judge and jury for the Fae. The Reapers carry out the punishments. Death chooses Fae based on their warrior skills and how they died. Each Reaper was betrayed in some way."

She swallowed and brought her legs up to her chest. "Okay."

"When a Fae becomes a Reaper, Death adds to their magic, making them extremely powerful. Bran was one of the first seven Reapers. But Death put strict rules in place. Once a Reaper pledges themselves to the part, they can have no contact with their family or friends in any way. They are prohibited from telling anyone who they are. And it is forbidden for a Reaper to fall in love."

"Because they're assassins and need to work in the shadows," Cat said with a nod. "The rules make sense."

Fintan found his gaze drawn to her. He stared into her green eyes, the sun glinting off the red strands of her hair. "Bran fell in love. Not only that, he told his Light Fae lover who he was. In response to the rules being broken, Death had no choice but to carry out the punishment. She killed the Light.

"Bran didn't take it well. He worked to turn Reaper against Reaper. Soon, they were divided. Bran and three others attacked the remaining three. He killed the leader first, and the three who sided with Bran were quickly slain."

Cat frowned. "Why didn't Death step in?"

"Death did and sent Bran into the Netherworld. It's a realm used as a Fae prison."

"But he didn't stay there."

Fintan shook his head slowly. "For thousands of years, he did. But he recently escaped with some help. His mission is to kill the Reapers—as well as Death."

"So why go after half-Fae?"

"He attempted to fool the Reapers by saying that Death ordered it, but the Reapers didn't fall for it. Bran and his army went after them instead."

Cat licked her lips. "Then what happened?"

"The Reapers tried to save as many Halflings as they could. Somehow, Bran has managed to pass on his power to his Dark army. It's seven Reapers against hundreds with the same added strength and magic."

"How many times have you fought Bran?"

"Three," he replied before he realized that he'd inadvertently told her he was a Reaper.

She shrugged and gave him a soft smile. "I knew as soon as you began speaking about the Reapers that you were one of them. Why didn't you just tell me?"

"You feared us."

"Perhaps, but that was before you helped me."

He blew out a breath as he turned to the sea. "I thought I was helping. Now I'm beginning to wonder if I've made things worse."

"It's easy to live in a pretend world," she said. "I did it for years. I pretended that I had magic just as my brother and sister did. Fantasizing hides the truth, and it's reality that I'd rather hold onto now."

He gazed into her eyes. "Reality sucks."

"Sometimes. But if I'm going to be in this, I need truth above all else. No matter how harsh it is. Regardless if you think I can handle it. I must have it."

He slowly released a breath. "Bran won't stop until he has you."

"What will happen if he wins against the Reapers and Death?"

"Chaos. We keep the balance between light and dark."

The breeze snagged a lock of her hair and blew it across her face. She tucked the strand behind her ear and turned to the waves crashing upon the shore. "You came to me because you knew I could help you draw Bran out. He believes he's smarter than us. Let's prove him wrong."

CHAPTER
eight

Cat wrapped herself in the heartache of losing her last family member. It would be her armor as she went after those responsible.

As Fintan told her about the Reapers and Bran, all the pieces came together. It hadn't taken long for her to realize that he was a Reaper. There had been a moment of panic. Then she looked at the facts.

He was there to help her.

He had given her a weapon to kill a Fae.

Bran had murdered her grandfather, brother, and sister.

If she was going to trust anyone, it was Fintan. There were few options for her, but she was betting everything on the white-haired Reaper.

"You should stay here," Fintan said.

She thought of the cottage that was warded against Fae as she turned her head to him. "It didn't help my grandfather. And you wouldn't be able to come inside."

"I can keep watch out here."

"You said Bran could remain veiled a long time. He could be watching us now."

Fintan blinked before slowly nodding. "He could. He could've had men watching you for weeks. But you don't stand a chance against him on your own."

"That's my point. He could kill me at any time. Why hasn't he?"

Lines creased Fintan's brow. "I don't know."

"Before you arrived. If he was here, why didn't he kill me? I wasn't hiding."

"Nay. You weren't."

It wasn't what he said that bothered her, but what he didn't. If Bran had the chance to kill her and refrained, that meant he had something else planned for her. And quite frankly, she didn't want to even think about what that could be.

She watched as Fintan rose and began to pace before her with long strides. Her gaze locked on his thighs and the way the muscles moved beneath his pants.

What made a man such as him? He was quiet, but was that a product of being an assassin, or was it his nature? He was aloof, but was that because his looks garnered such attention?

She wanted to know his story. He'd said every Reaper was betrayed and that led to their death. Someone had deceived him. That left a deep scar upon a person.

Her thoughts then turned to his death. Had it been painful? Had he suffered? It shouldn't matter. He was a Reaper now. In the end, he'd won.

Hadn't he?

Suddenly, her story didn't seem so sad anymore. Who cared that she didn't have magic? She was alive. She hadn't been betrayed. It was a wonder Fintan hadn't laughed in her face as she spoke of her troubles.

They were nothing compared to what he'd endured.

His long, white hair was ruffled by the breeze, but he appeared unfazed as he continued to think. Most likely about Bran. She might've heard the story now, but she still didn't understand Bran.

It was easy to discern his motivations, however. Revenge.

Though that seemed too simple. Fintan painted Bran as a power-hungry Fae with a god complex. Bran might be after more than just vengeance.

As if her thoughts about Bran had conjured him, Searlas appeared behind Fintan.

"Behind you!" Cat shouted.

Fintan ducked as an orb of magic was thrown his way. Two more Dark appeared and attacked. She jumped up, looking around as she waited for someone to come for her.

She was an easy target now that Fintan was otherwise engaged. But there was no one. She then turned her attention to Fintan ... and was awed.

The closest she'd come to seeing a fight was on the tele, but here it was, just yards in front of her. The grunts and the sounds of magic meeting flesh filled the air.

Her eyes widened when Fintan elbowed one of the Dark in the throat before he leaned back to miss an orb thrown by Searlas. As nimble as Fintan was, and as good as his defense, it was still three against one.

She gasped when a ball of magic slammed into his hip. It disintegrated his pants and sank into his flesh, leaving a black ring that looked extremely painful.

Yet Fintan didn't so much as acknowledge it. He used his

entire body as a weapon from his feet to his head. The speed with which he moved was impossible to track.

She wondered why he didn't have his sword. He could end them quickly with the blade. Then her neck began to tingle. It was the feeling that someone was watching her.

Cat slowly turned to look over her shoulder to find a Fae with long, black hair, standing near the cottage. He smiled and held out his hand for her.

There was no need to ask who he was. It was Bran. Though when he didn't kill her right then, it confirmed her fear that he wanted something from her. If only she had the dagger Fintan had procured for her. She would plunge it into Bran's black heart and smile while doing it. But it still sat on her kitchen table.

She fisted her hand, then looked down in shock as she felt something in her palm. There, as clear as day, was the weapon. She turned around and rushed to help Fintan.

Leaping onto a Dark who held a ball of magic against Fintan's back, she plunged the blade into the Dark's neck.

The next instant, he was nothing but dust. Before she could move to the next, Searlas gripped her wrist that held the dagger. His red eyes blazed as he leaned down to look at her.

"Take Bran's offer."

"Kiss off," she said and twisted out of his grip.

When she turned around, Searlas was holding Fintan down with a huge orb of magic aimed at his face. Arms of steel locked around her from behind, preventing her from going to help Fintan.

Her gaze met the Reaper's. He gave her a small nod of encouragement. He was telling her she could do it, that she could fight against her attacker and win. It was all the reinforcement she needed.

She leaned forward before swinging her head back and slamming it into her attacker's face. The Dark released her with a spew of obscenities. She quickly pivoted and thrust the dagger up into the Fae's stomach. Red eyes widened in disbelief before he turned to dust.

Breathing heavily, Cat whirled around, ready to toss Fintan the dagger. Except Fintan used his strength and slowly turned the orb toward Searlas. It came closer and closer to Searlas's face. Just before it touched him, Searlas gave a bellow and vanished.

She looked to the cottage, but there was no sign of Bran. She and Fintan were the only two people on the beach. The battle was over, and yet her heart wouldn't stop pounding, and her grip on the dagger didn't ease.

Fintan got to his feet and walked to her. His shirt was in tatters, barely hanging on to his body. His pants were ripped and burned from the magic.

She feasted upon the glimpses of skin and rippling muscle she was allowed to see. She'd sensed there was power beneath the clothes, power that had nothing to do with magic. Her gaze ran back up his body to his face.

There was something in his eyes, something that made the bloodlust turn to hunger. She took a step toward him and then another until they were within inches of each other.

She lifted her face, waiting for his kiss. Yearning for it. Something in her had changed. She didn't know when or how, but it had. And she welcomed it.

His large hand came around to her lower back, holding her as he took her mouth in a kiss that stole her breath as much as it made her burn.

She wound her arms around his neck and parted her lips. His

tongue swept in. The taste of him made her shiver. Her sex clenched as desire pulsed.

As quickly as the kiss had begun, it ended. He released her and took a step back. She fought to remain upright after such an incredible, astonishing kiss that was entirely too short.

His white eyes burned with palpable hunger. She wanted him, too. So why was he putting up walls between them?

"I saw Bran," he said.

She nodded, the words lodged in her throat.

"He didn't take you."

Cat blinked and looked down at her arms. They were covered in blood. That's when she realized that she had blood splattered all over her.

"Odd," Fintan continued. "Searlas spoke to you. What did he say?"

She lifted her eyes to Fintan. His gaze was clear, calm. Had she imagined the desire? The kiss?

The need?

"He wanted me to take Bran's offer," she finally said.

Fintan frowned deeply. "What offer?"

"I don't know."

"Have you seen Bran before today?"

She shook her head and walked past him toward the cottage.

"Think carefully," he said as he fell into step behind her. "He could've disguised himself. Have you gotten any type of offers lately?"

"No. He held out his hand to me, and I went to help you."

Fintan made a sound at the back of his throat. "Bran could've killed you right then. I don't believe he made a mistake. He wants you for something."

She whirled around and held up the dagger so that the point touched his chest. "My only thought was to help you."

"I can take care of myself."

"Yes," she said and looked pointedly at the burns on his body that were even now healing. "I'll remember that next time. Trust me, I won't think twice about wanting to help you again."

As she went to turn around, he grabbed her arm, causing the point of the dagger to pierce his skin. A bead of blood appeared and rolled down his chest.

She followed the bright red droplet as it made its way over the thick sinew of his pecs to his chiseled abs. Her lips tingled from their kiss while her body ached to feel him against her once more.

"When did you get the blade?" he demanded.

She lifted her chin as she looked into his white eyes. "I don't know. I saw Bran and wished I had it so I could use it on him. Next thing I knew, it was in my hand. Perhaps I should've gone after him and let you get an orb to the face."

Their gazes remained locked together for several tense minutes before he loosened his grip. "You did good today."

With her anger cooling, she glanced down at the weapon. Confusion marred her visage as she kept trying to figure out how it had ended up in her hand. "Then why don't I feel better about any of this?"

"Because you recognize what's at stake."

She pulled her arm from his grip and lowered the dagger. "Do I?" She wasn't so sure about that.

Without another word, she pivoted and made her way to the cottage. It had been a sanctuary for her once. A place where she could be surrounded by love and happiness—and safety.

Now, it would stand as a monument to the last member of her family.

She stood at the doorway of the house, but she didn't go inside. How could she now without her grandfather? Always wise, forever full of kindness. There would never be another like him.

In the distance, she could hear the sirens of approaching authorities. Someone else had finally seen the smoke. Her world as she knew it was over.

Now, she was moving into one of battle and blood. One of magic and betrayal. She was ill-prepared for such a role. She had no battle training, nor any magic.

She might end up a liability, but she was going to give it everything she had. For her family.

For herself.

She didn't need to turn around to know that Fintan was behind her. She could sense his presence. "If they see you, it'll raise questions."

"I'm not leaving you."

Turning, she held out the dagger for him. "Hold this for me."

"Cat—"

"This is human business now," she interrupted him. "I need to take care of this."

With a nod, he disappeared. She was sure he'd simply veiled himself because she could still sense him near. Oddly, that gave her the courage to face what came next.

Then she remembered the blood she had on her. No one could see her like this. As she lifted her hands, her mind racing for how to fix her clothes, there was a sizzle along her skin.

It was soft, soothing even. As she looked, the blood vanished from her skin and clothes.

"Thank you," she whispered to Fintan as the first of the cars arrived.

CHAPTER

nine

Grief dulled Cat's eyes as she dealt with the authorities for over two hours, answering endless questions. Fintan was veiled and never more than five feet from her during it all.

Through everything, Cat stood strong. Her gaze often turned to the cottage, and he could guess that memories of the past haunted her.

Fintan wasn't surprised by Bran's move against the old man. What worried him was this so-called offer from Bran to Cat. No matter how Fintan wracked his brain, he couldn't discern what Bran might want with Cat.

And that only magnified his anxiety.

He didn't want to bring other Reapers into this, but he may not have a choice. Once more, Bran had changed tactics. Instead of trying to kill the Halfling, he had a proposition for her instead.

If only Fintan could learn what that was, then he might be able to help Cat. Until he discovered Bran's motives, they were once more fighting blind.

For eons, no one had come close to the Reapers in power and strength. Now, one stood in their way that disrupted everything. Fintan didn't fear for himself. He'd lived and died once before—and was prepared to do so again.

No, his thoughts were on his brethren.

And Cat.

Already, one of his brothers was lost. Eoghan could be dead, or he could be suffering horribly while they fought to end Bran. All the while, Bran continually changed his attacks and intentions, leaving the Reapers guessing.

Fintan's plan to lure Bran and capture him had been flawless. It should've worked. Instead, it had backfired. Cat had lost her business and her grandfather in the span of an hour.

But Bran hadn't tried to kill her.

Fintan ran a hand down his face. In his other hand was the dagger he'd given her. He still didn't know how she'd managed to call it to her.

For someone who supposedly didn't have magic, she had used a magical ability.

There was something at work here that he couldn't decipher, something that prevented him from seeing a clear picture of things.

If he knew Cat would go into the cottage and remain, Fintan would travel to Inchmickery. But he knew to leave her would be folly.

"Cael," he whispered.

As a rule, the Reapers always veiled themselves when they teleported. So it was easy for him to spot Cael as soon as he arrived. The leader of the Reapers made his way over, weaving among the humans.

Cael stopped beside him, crossing his arms over his chest as they watched the scene. "What happened?"

"Bran attacked Cat's grandfather after they burned her café this morning."

One black brow rose. "So your plan worked. How close are you to killing him?"

"Not as close as I'd like."

"Meaning?"

Fintan blew out a breath as they took several steps back so the humans wouldn't overhear them. "Bran changed his tactics. I fought Searlas and two others. During that, Bran showed up."

"Did he approach Cat?"

"No."

Cael's frowned deepened as he waited for the rest.

"Searlas told Cat to take Bran's offer," Fintan said.

Cael's head jerked his way. "Offer?" he asked, interests piqued. "What offer?"

"I don't know. Neither does Cat. She said she's not had anyone approach her with any kind of proposition."

With his gaze lowered to the sand, Cael asked, "What is the bastard about now?"

"Bran had the opportunity to kill Cat today, but he didn't. He wants her for something."

"That can't be good."

"I'm not leaving Cat's side until we figure this out."

Cael's gaze lifted to meet his. Then he gave a slow nod as he dropped his arms to his sides. "Agreed. What do you need from me?"

"See if there are any other Halflings who Bran hasn't killed. There could be a pattern."

"Or this could be about Cat in particular."

Fintan glanced at her, shaking his head. "She has no magic."

"You said that with more conviction yesterday. What happened?"

He looked at the blade now clean of blood. "I gave this weapon to Cat this morning. Yesterday, she asked for something to protect herself since she has no magic."

"And the problem?"

"She said she's the only one in her family to ever be born without magic. She's convinced of it. I also don't sense any magic within her."

Cael's gaze narrowed. "But?"

"I'd just given her the dagger when the call came in about the fire at the café. Once we returned to her cottage, she saw the smoke here. I teleported us to save time."

"So the weapon was left behind."

"Precisely," Fintan said with a nod.

Cael raised a brow. "By your look, I take it you didn't return for it?"

"Cat used it to kill one of the Dark I was fighting."

Crossing his arms over his chest, Cael glanced at Cat before turning his head back to Fintan. "If she left it, how did it get here?"

Fintan lowered the weapon against his leg. "She told me when she saw Bran, she wished she had it, and then it was in her hand."

"Any way you look at it, that's magic."

"I know." Fintan blew out a breath.

Cael dropped his arms. "I understand your dilemma. It worries me because I don't sense magic within her either. If that's the case, what could she offer Bran?"

"I've been trying to figure that out."

"I'll get the others working to see what we can find," Cael said.

"What about Eoghan? Anything?" he asked before Cael could teleport away.

Cael sighed, his chin dropping to his chest. "Still nothing. It's like he never was."

"Only Death could do something like that. I knew Bran was powerful, but I didn't think his magic had reached that magnitude."

"Neither did I." Cael ran a hand through his long, black hair and raised his head. "We won't stop looking. Ever. If Eoghan is out there, we will find him."

"Will he be the same?"

"We'll deal with that when the time comes. For now, we've our regular duties on top of stopping Bran, finding Eoghan, and now looking for more Halflings."

Fintan knew how overworked everyone was. "How are the girls?"

The girls being Jordyn, River, and Neve, who had joined the ranks of the Reapers—though Neve was the only true Reaper of the three.

She'd joined her mate, Talin, as a team. In the short time that she'd been with them, she'd become a great asset. In truth, Fintan had doubted any of the girls could help. He was happy to be proven wrong.

"They're all doing their parts," Cael said. "Kyran is adjusting to River's mood swings as the baby grows in her womb."

Fintan grunted at the news. One of the most feared Dark,

Kyran now doted on the half-Fae that was his mate and mother of his child.

"I never saw us on this path," Fintan said.

Cael shook his head. "Neither did I. Though you won't have to worry about me falling in love."

"My stand goes without saying. What about Daire?"

"I think he's falling for Rhi."

The legendary Light Fae who'd once had a torrid affair with a Dragon King was now Death's focus. Erith had sent Daire to follow Rhi everywhere.

"That won't end well," Fintan said. "Everyone knows Rhi is still in love with her Dragon King."

"Hopefully, Daire is smarter than that—knows better than to give his heart to her."

"And if he's not?"

Cael shrugged. "I no longer see the road before us. It's crumbled and overrun."

"We'll prevail. We have Death on our side."

When Cael didn't respond, Fintan looked closely at him. There was something his leader wasn't telling them. He'd allow Cael his secrets—for now.

There would come a time soon enough when everything would come out in the open. And though Cael was always quiet when it came to them discussing Death, there was an added layer there now. Fintan could sense it.

It was as if Cael were intentionally clamming up and hoping no one would notice. Could this have something to do with Bran escaping the Netherworld? After all, Death had made the doorway to the prison.

That doorway should have only been visible to her. Yet Seamus had found it. The Dark Fae had then opened it and allowed Bran to flee.

Either Seamus had as much magic as Death—which was highly unlikely—or there was something wrong with Erith. Fintan was leaning toward the latter.

Whatever it was, Cael was dealing with it. When—and if—their leader needed them, Cael would let them know. Until then, Fintan knew he could shoulder whatever it was. Otherwise, Cael wouldn't be leading them.

"What else have you learned about Cat?" Cael asked.

Fintan's gaze found her standing next to the body of her grandfather that was now in a black bag being rolled away to a van. "She's strong-willed. She has an amazing amount of courage despite what she's facing and everything she's lost."

"Do you trust her?"

"You mean, do I think she's playing me? Nay, I don't. I think she fears for her life, but she's prepared to do whatever it takes to get revenge on Bran for what he's done."

"Good."

"I told her about us." Death already knew since she stayed apprised of her Reapers, so he didn't feel the need to keep it from Cael.

Cael blew out a breath. "The rules have changed for us. I'm not sure what Death will do. Right now, keep Cat alive."

"That goes without saying."

Cael's head leaned to the side as he stared at him. "There's something different about you."

"Nay."

"Aye," he argued. "It's in your eyes. It's as if you're worried."

Fintan looked away from Cael's prying gaze. "You know I have no emotions."

"Of course."

He didn't release his breath until Cael was gone. It shook him that Cael could see the concern that had been growing within him since Eoghan had disappeared in that vortex of magic.

Allowing that little bit of emotion in had opened him up to much more. Cat was a prime example. There was no denying the desire he felt for her.

Something within made him wonder at lust ruling him in such a way. Or could it be something ... more?

It ate at him, gnawing at his control day and night. The kiss had been a terrible, amazing mistake. Now he knew just how wonderful she tasted, how hot her passion burned.

Giving in to that lust had been the worst thing he could have done because now the essence of her was in him. It added to his longing, making it impossible for him to keep his emotions firmly locked away.

He ached to hold her against him again, to feel her soft body in his arms. Even now, he could hear the way she moaned into his mouth at the first brush of his tongue against hers.

She was a temptation he dared not allow himself to have. Yet, he yearned for everything she had to offer.

With an iron will forged during his time as the Dark King's right hand, Fintan slowly turned off any and all emotion. It was the only way he would be able to get through what was coming with Cat.

Already, he'd begun to feel something for her, and in this war, that was dangerous. For her sake—and his—he would do what was needed.

There could never be anything between them. He was a Reaper, who would always go by the original rules Death had put in place for them. A Reaper couldn't do his job if his heart belonged to someone.

And Fintan was a Reaper—nothing more, nothing less. His role meant everything to him. He wouldn't allow anything to destroy what he now had.

Not even a Halfling as beautiful as Catriona Hayes.

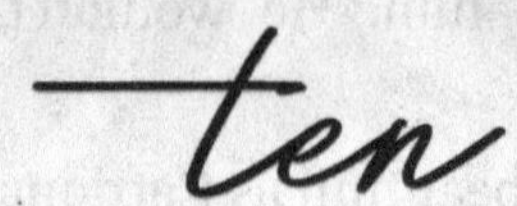

Cat wasn't sure why she remained at the beach. Perhaps it was to see if Bran would come for her. Or maybe it was because she couldn't bear to leave yet.

Her family may not have been large, but never had she thought she would be the only surviving member. She felt like a tiny speck of dust, and the Earth seemed as large as the universe.

Though Fintan was near, he hadn't shown himself or spoken since the authorities arrived. She was glad since she wasn't in the mood to carry on a conversation. Her grief was just too great. It weighed her down, crushing her.

For hours, she stood at the shoreline. The tide went out and came back in. The sun made its way across the sky and was now sinking into the horizon.

Life teemed around her as if a person hadn't been viciously murdered. But then again, that was the way of the world. People focused on themselves instead of noticing others' pain.

She might want the world to stop, but the fact was that it

wouldn't—it couldn't. Even after her parents' sudden deaths, her grandfather had made her and her siblings continue on, forcing them to look to the future.

He'd done the same thing to her when her brother and sister were killed. And she knew if her grandfather could talk to her now, he'd tell her to carry on.

Because she must.

The wind grew colder. It stung her cheeks, and though she felt it, she didn't care. Inside, she couldn't decide if she wanted to curl in a ball and cry, grow numb about everything, or let vengeance rule her.

The week before, she and her grandfather had talked about how weird the holidays would be with just the two of them now. If she managed to survive this war, she would be celebrating alone.

"Enough."

She closed her eyes as she heard Fintan's voice. A large jacket was draped around her. In the next heartbeat, she was lifted in his arms. She didn't fight him. Instead, she rested her head on his shoulder. A second later, she found herself inside her home. He strode to the bathroom where the shower was already on, steam filling the area.

He set her down in the tub and jerked the shower curtain closed. Before her clothes grew soggy, they vanished. She could only shake her head at the magic of a Fae.

As soon as the hot water met her skin, she realized how cold she was. She moved beneath the spray, wrapping her arms around herself and letting the water heat her.

Once most of the shaking had stopped, she washed. Not once did she dare to peek around the curtain. She both hoped—and dreaded—that he was there.

After she had turned off the water, she reached for the towel hanging on the hook. A quick glance confirmed that she was alone. There was a surge of disappointment that she hastily shoved aside.

Toweling off, she put on sweats and ran her fingers through her hair before she walked out of the room. Fintan was standing beside the kitchen table, his hand on the back of a chair as he waited for her.

Cat made her way to him and sank into the chair. She took a deep breath and smelled something delicious. Her stomach rumbled, reminding her that she hadn't eaten at all that day.

He then set a bowl of soup before her. "Eat."

She really hated bossy men. At least, she normally did. At that moment, she was thankful for him. He could've left her to her own devices, but he hadn't. He'd given her time, and when he deemed it enough, had taken matters into his own hands.

No words were spoken as she ate, and he sat across from her. It wasn't until she'd finished her second bowl that she pushed it away and looked at him.

"Now what?" she asked.

He raised a white brow. "When I told you we tried to save Halflings, we succeeded. Baylon found Jordyn in Edinburgh. She was just setting out, finding anything she could on the Fae. He was there to save her when Bran came to kill her. In doing so, they fell in love."

That wasn't what she'd expected from the story. "That's against Death's rules. Was she killed?"

"Death realized history was repeating itself. We all recognized that. It was Jordyn's quick thinking that helped us with Bran. Maybe that's what ultimately swayed Death because the rules changed. Baylon and Jordyn were allowed to remain together—with the rest of the Reapers."

"Oh." She couldn't imagine how that must have happened. "Were the rest of you all right with that decision?"

He gave her a confused look. "We didn't have to kill Jordyn or Baylon. We were ecstatic. I'll not lie and say it wasn't odd to have a female among us, though."

"I bet," she said with a grin.

His white eyes held hers. "We discovered that Bran was after a set of books. When Kyran and Talin broke into the library in Edinburgh, they found that someone had been gathering the books we needed to keep from Bran. That person was a half-Fae named River.

"She fought my brothers to keep the books protected. Kyran and Talin took the volumes anyway. It wasn't until we tried to read them that we realized each was in a different Fae language that hadn't been spoken in millions of years."

Cat leaned forward, resting her arms on the table. "Could Bran read them?"

"I don't know. Somehow, Kyran put it together that River could. It took some doing, but we talked her into helping us. Though she has no magic, she has the ability to understand any and all Fae languages. However, her willingness to help us put her on Bran's radar. He went after her."

"Please tell me you protected River."

He took a deep breath and released it. "We did. In the midst of it all, Kyran fell in love with her, and she now carries his child."

Cat's eyes widened. "That's amazing. I guess Death allowed her to remain, as well?"

"We have need of River. And no one wanted a repeat of history."

"Besides," Cat said with a twist of her lips. "Baylon got to keep his woman."

Fintan nodded. "Exactly. Two Halflings who were targeted by Bran to die."

"I see a pattern."

"We all did. Death's next move was to send Talin to the court of the Light Fae to spy on those there. He'd been doing it for months. What we didn't know was that Bran also had a spy among them. As soon as Talin showed an interest in a female, Bran went after Neve. He killed her parents in front of her and turned her brother Dark."

Cat might only be half-Fae, but she knew what that meant to a Light. Cat couldn't imagine the horror Neve must have felt.

"Neve tried to save her brother with the help of a Light Fae named Rhi. They both thought once away from Bran that Atris would return to his old self. Only, he killed Neve."

Cat's hand covered her mouth as Fintan's words registered.

He looked to the table and sat there for a moment. "What we all knew was that Talin had fallen in love with Neve. Death made concessions for Halflings, but not for a Fae. That rule didn't change."

Cat closed her eyes, unsure if she could hear more. The Reapers were supposed to be powerful. Death was ... well, Death. Something should've been done.

"Neve was betrayed and killed," Fintan said.

That's when it hit her. She snapped opened her eyes and lowered her hand. "Neve became a Reaper."

"Yes."

"Three Reapers have found love and gotten to live. That's good," she said with a smile.

But Fintan didn't return it.

Then she frowned as she recalled something he'd said before. "Seven. There are seven of you. Neve would make eight."

"It would, but the night she was killed, there was a great battle between the Reapers and Bran's army. Rhi joined us. It was her magic that stopped Bran's, but the consequence was a vicious swirling storm of magic.

"Bran managed to control it, pointing it at Cael, who was wounded. Eoghan, one of the original Reapers, pushed Cael out of the way, and in the process, was sucked into the storm."

One of Fintan's friends was missing. She reached across and laid her hand atop his. "Is Eoghan dead?"

"We don't believe so, but we've yet to find him. We won't stop looking until we do."

She looked down at her hand against his and slowly sat back, releasing him. "And Rhi? She's a Fae. Does she know who you are?"

"Death wiped her memories."

"Why not kill her?"

"The same reason Death has Daire following her. We don't know."

Cat chuckled. "And who questions Death, right?"

"Exactly."

"Why did you tell me all of this?"

He rubbed a hand over his jaw and glanced away. "In all three cases, Bran has tried to kill the females. I assumed since he murdered your brother and sister that he would do the same to you."

"But?" she urged when he paused.

"He had ample opportunity to kill you today, and he didn't."

She blew out a breath. "The offer, you mean?"

"There's one out there. You received it, though you might not remember it."

Cat rose and put her bowl in the sink. When she turned back

around, she braced her hands on either side of her on the counter. "When I saw Bran today, I instinctively knew it was him. It was like I knew him."

"He was probably the one who approached you with the proposition."

"When you spoke of him, I thought he'd turned Dark after all of his kills."

Fintan stood and pushed in the chair. "When we became Reapers, we ceased being Light or Dark. We became what Death created, though we keep the coloring we had in life."

"I've already told you I haven't seen Bran before today."

"But you recognized him."

She scrunched up her face, unable to deny the truth. "Yes, but I don't know how."

"You get many customers in your café each day. You can't remember them all."

She shot him a flat look. "I remember Fae."

"Then he used magic."

"That doesn't make me feel any better."

"It shouldn't," Fintan said. He turned and looked at the curtains that were closed over the front window.

Cat pushed away from the counter and walked to stand before him. "If you hadn't been here, I wouldn't have known about Bran. I wouldn't know he was the one responsible for killing my brother and sister."

"You would've seen the evil in him."

"You sound so sure of that, but I'm not. His offer might have been similar to yours. Maybe he wants to protect me. I would've accepted that."

Fintan's white eyes blazed with intensity. "You've been around Fae your entire life. Do you know when one uses glamour?"

She shrugged, scrunching up her face. "A few instances it seems as if there's just something not quite right with a Fae."

"You would've seen through Bran."

"Before it was too late?"

He held her gaze for a moment longer. "Why are you worrying about something that didn't happen?"

"I don't know."

"You've had a rough day," he said and stepped aside. With a hand on her back, he ushered her to the door to her bedroom. "You need to rest. Everything will be clearer in the morning."

"I doubt it," she mumbled but walked to her bed and curled beneath the covers.

CHAPTER

eleven

"I thought you said she'd come with you," Searlas said.

Bran looked at his lieutenant from his position slouched in the chair before the crackling fire. The manor they had commandeered was spacious, if somewhat ostentatious for his liking. But it was a place for them to rest.

A location the Reapers would never to think to look. Though it wasn't as if Cael or the other Reapers could track him. A complication the Reapers had yet to realize.

Searlas stared at him expectantly.

Bran stretched his legs out before him and crossed his ankles. "It's only a matter of time before Catriona comes with us."

"You still believe that even though Fintan is with her?"

"The Halfling is detrimental to our plans. I'm going to make sure she had no other option but to choose us."

Searlas poured himself a glass of whisky and joined Bran by the fire. "Even after we burned her café?"

"Who says we did it?" Bran asked with a grin.

"Brilliant."

Bran shrugged. "I always get what I want. And right now, I want Catriona Hayes."

"Do you think Fintan and the others know what she's capable of?"

"If they did, they'd take her someplace I'd never be able to get to. All Fintan was concerned with was trying to trap me. He's not looking at the Halfling as he should be."

"That's to our advantage," Searlas stated.

Bran held up his glass of whisky to see the firelight through it. "Don't underestimate the Reapers. To do that will be our downfall."

"But we're ahead."

His gaze swung to Searlas. "Ahead? I told you when you joined me that my goals meant it would be a long campaign."

"I understand that, but we killed Eoghan."

"What makes you think that?"

"The magic swallowed him," Searlas stated as if he were talking to a daft person.

Bran sometimes forgot that his lieutenant saw only two sides and missed everything in between. Searlas was a loyal fighter but was a few sheep short of a flock at times.

"That magic was a combination of mine and that Light Fae's— whoever the feck she is. I don't know what our combined power created, but Eoghan isn't dead. All I knew is that I wanted Cael gone. And he would be if Eoghan hadn't pushed him out of the way."

"How do you know Eoghan is still alive?" Searlas asked with a frown.

Bran scratched his eyebrow. "I just do."

"I was hoping he'd be dead."

"It'll come," Bran said with a smile. "Patience, Searlas. It's what got me out of the Netherworld. It's what has allowed me to syphon Erith's magic. And it will grant my goals."

Searlas finished his whisky and smacked his lips together. "Despite the Reapers gaining the books we needed and preventing us from killing all the Halflings?"

"I'll admit, the Reapers gaining the books is a hindrance. We needed those, but with Catriona, we'll be able to get them. As for the Halflings? Let the Reapers believe they've saved them."

"Oh, how I love the way your mind works," Searlas said with a laugh.

Bran smiled and took a sip of the fine Irish whisky. "The Reapers are down by one with Eoghan gone. They'll be searching for him and worried about trapping me. They won't have a clue what's coming next."

"I almost wish I could see their faces when they discover what they had right before them this whole time."

"I never thought any of them would realize Catriona existed. I was about to give up on my plan." Bran pressed the side of the glass against this temple. "I should've known it would be Fintan."

Searlas gave a loud snort. "The fekker is too devoid of emotion to gain the Halfling's trust."

"You sure about that?"

Searlas nodded rapidly. "Definitely."

"And yet she fought alongside him today. I'd almost call it defending him."

"She did kill one of ours," Searlas said with a frown.

Bran raised a brow. "Do you still hold to your original opinion that Fintan won't gain any trust with Cat?"

"If you think he's gaining ground, why not go to her now?"

"What would be the fun in that?"

Searlas shook his head as he sat back in the chair. "And if the Halfling falls for Fintan?"

"Then her betrayal will cut him even deeper when she comes to me."

"Are you sure about this?" Talin asked.

Cael stood amid the tall trees of the Dragonwood and shook his head. "Nay, but since a Dragon King saw Fintan in Edinburgh, and you popped onto their land, I don't see how we have a choice."

"Not to mention, they're discussing us anyway."

There was that. Daire had told them of the gathering of the Dragon Kings and Rhi, as they talked about not only the Reapers but also Con's affair with the Light Queen, Usaeil.

Cael decided not to put Con on the defensive and show up in his office, though it would've made things easier. He looked to the sky. At one time, dragons would've been flying overhead the moment someone breached the magical barrier around Dreagan.

But the Dark's release of the video of the Kings shifting had put too much focus on the secretive and reclusive dragons. Cael didn't blame the Kings' initial reaction of pulling down the video, but he might've done things differently.

Then again, it was easy for him to say such things since he was looking at it from a different angle rather than being right in the mix with everything he held dear on the line.

"Who are you?" demanded a deep voice behind them.

Talin spun around. Cael slowly turned and came face-to-face with Constantine, King of Dragon Kings. He looked into Con's black eyes as snow flurries danced around them.

"Well, shite," said a man who walked up behind Con and saw Talin.

Talin nodded his head. "Roman."

Con never looked away from Cael. "I asked who you were."

"Reapers." Cael decided to get right to the point. "My name is Cael, and I lead them."

A blond brow arched as Con glanced at Talin. "It's no' a coincidence you showing up claiming to be Reapers after we were just talking about you, is it?"

"We're not claiming anything," Talin said.

Cael shook his head, spotting another Dragon King off to his right. "No, it isn't. I came for several reasons. The first was to let you know that Usaeil had pictures of you two posted all over the Light Castle."

"I'm aware."

Roman crossed his arms over his chest. "And the other reason?"

"Talin made a mistake in showing himself to you. I'd intended our first meeting to occur differently," Cael said.

Con looked around the forest, touching the trees as he walked past them to move closer to Cael. "And the white-haired Fae Darius saw in Edinburgh? Am I to assume he's a Reaper?"

Cael nodded. "Fintan is one of us, aye."

"Why are you showing yourselves to us now?" Con asked.

"We work for Death," Cael explained. "Death is judge and jury and keeps the balance between our kind. We're the executioners. Our identities are kept from all Fae, but there is an imbalance that hasn't been righted yet. Which is why I'm here."

Roman blew out a harsh breath and gave a shake of his sandy blond head. "Where were you during the Fae Wars?"

"On assignment elsewhere," Talin stated.

Cael shrugged one shoulder. "There are seven of us. Or were. We're battling an ex-Reaper named Bran, who escaped from a Fae prison realm and is seeking retribution."

"And this matters to us why?" Roman asked.

Cael glanced at the Dragon King before returning his gaze to Con. "Because it's only a matter of time before Bran turns his attention on you. You're battling the Dark. Bran is recruiting the Dark."

"Why should that worry us?" Con questioned.

"For a variety of reasons. The first being that when we accept Death's offer to become a Reaper, our magic triples. We're faster, stronger, and can remain veiled for as long as we want. Bran is somehow giving those same benefits to the Dark he recruits."

"And they don't stay dead," Talin added.

Roman gawked at him as his arms fell to his sides. "Surely you're exaggerating a wee bit."

"We kill Bran's men, but they just keep coming back to life," Talin explained.

Con drew in a breath and released it. "I gather since Death isna doing anything that this entity isna able?"

"Death is fighting back."

Roman barked a laugh. "It's Death. Judge and jury are what you said. Why can Death no' just smite Bran where he stands."

"Because, somehow, Bran's appearance has affected Death," Con said.

Cael ignored Talin's intense look and gave a quick nod. "Something like that. I wanted you to know of us, and to warn you about Usaeil. Watch out for her."

A weary look briefly flashed in Con's black eyes. "I'm taking care of her. Give me the names of all the Reapers."

"Me," Cael said. "Talin, Kyran, Daire, Baylon, Fintan, Eoghan, and Neve."

Con tilted his head slightly. "That's eight."

"We had a new edition recently."

Roman asked, "How does Death choose a Reaper?"

"We're warriors, who have been betrayed and killed," Talin said. "Death then finds us."

"So there's only you eight—or seven since one of you is missing—right?" Con asked.

Cael forced himself to smile since the reminder of Eoghan's disappearance was always one that hit him hard. "Yes."

"And why is Bran no longer a Reaper?"

"One of Death's rules is that we can't have any sort of relationship with family, friends, or ... anyone, for that matter. Another is that if a Fae discovers who we are, they have to die. Bran fell in love with a Light Fae and told her who he was."

Con dislodged the snow from his hair when he raked a hand through it. "So, Death had no choice but to kill the Light Fae, which in turn caused Bran to get angry."

"Pretty much," Talin said.

Cael held out his hand to watch the snow pile on his palm. "Bran divided us. It was his four Reapers against my three. He managed to execute our leader and another of us. Eoghan and I fought for our lives, which meant we had to kill two of our brothers. Then Death arrived and took Bran to the Netherworld."

"Leaving Cael and Eoghan," Talin said. "Death built the next set of Reapers around them."

Con said, "How much do you know about us?"

"Enough to know that the story of Bran isn't that much different than Ulrik's."

There was a stretch of silence before Con turned to Roman. "You and Cain return to the manor."

Roman gave a nod and turned on his heel to walk away. Cael saw the other King disappear over the rise of a hill. Then he turned to Talin and said, "Return to the isle. I'll follow soon."

Talin bowed his head to Con before teleporting away.

Cael looked at the King of Kings. "You have no reason to trust me, but I hope you will. We could both use allies."

"With enemies seemingly closing in from everywhere, I admit an ally could be useful."

"But?" Cael asked when Con paused.

"I only have your word for who you are."

Cael clasped his hands behind his back and smiled. "Then I'll prove it to you and earn your trust."

"How?"

"I'll have to figure that out. Until next time, King of Kings," Cael said and teleported away.

CHAPTER
twelve

The quiet seeped into every wall and corner of the house. It was almost a living, breathing entity. Normally, Fintan preferred silence, embracing it over the clamor of others. But he could find no solace in it this night.

He knew the cause.

Cat. Around her, the calm he'd worked so hard to achieve was stripped away, leaving him exposed ... unmasked. She was a storm upon his senses and long-dead emotions, causing him to be helplessly tossed and twisted about.

The pure, unadulterated lust that thrummed through his veins kept his body heated and achy. While the concern and—dare he even think it—fear kept him on edge.

His mind kept returning to their kiss. Her reaction had been instant and full of passion. The only thing he'd wanted was to lay her down on the sand and make long, sweet love to her.

That singular, surprising thought was what broke through his fog of yearning, enabling him to come to his senses enough to end the kiss.

He rose from his place at the kitchen table and walked around the house, putting up shields to keep any Fae but a Reaper out. He also looked for anything to distract his thoughts.

Then he found it.

On a bookshelf, he spotted some photo albums. Several minutes passed as he stared at them, debating whether to look through them. Finally, his curiosity won out, and he chose one. Taking it back to the sofa, he sat and opened the album.

Picture after picture of Cat graced the pages. From the day of her birth to holidays, birthdays, family trips, and school functions.

He saw moments of her laughing with her parents and opening Christmas presents alongside her siblings. Moments where she looked deep in thought, and even one where she was off to the side, sitting with a forlorn expression on her face as she watched her siblings doing magic.

Getting a glimpse of Cat in the photos was almost like him being a part of her life. He flipped through the pages eagerly, soaking up everything he could about her. It was the picture of her just a few years earlier at the beach with her grandfather that struck him. There was such happiness in her gaze that Fintan almost didn't recognize her.

Feeling as if he'd peeked into her life like a thief, he softly closed the album and rose to put it away. But shelving the photos didn't put her out of his mind. In fact, she was all he could think about.

Seemingly unable to do anything else, he walked down the hall to Cat's room. He opened the door and looked to her bed, but she wasn't in it. He found her sitting on the window seat with her legs pulled up to her chest. She wore a short nightgown that bared her shapely legs.

Her head swiveled to him. He saw the tears upon her cheeks, and it was like a sucker punch to his gut. All his life, he'd been a killer, a Fae sent to snuff out life. He was all that was harsh and cruel and abrasive. He didn't know the first thing about softness or grief.

But when he tried to back out of the room, his feet wouldn't obey.

Fintan walked to Cat and sat beside her. She rested her chin on her knees and blinked up at him. The moonlight glinted off her wet, spikey eyelashes. Her despair gutted him, shattered him.

For the second time in his life, he wanted to offer comfort—if only he knew how.

He didn't know the words, or even if he should touch her. Hadn't he seen a mother put an arm around a crying child? Surely, touching was the right thing to do.

But the more he thought about it, the more uncertain he became. Yet he couldn't sit there and do nothing. He lifted his hand, only to fist it in frustration. How he hated to be so indecisive.

Finally, he came to a decision and rested his hand atop her bare foot before he leaned back against the window. As he wracked his mind for some soothing words, she sniffed and scooted toward him, shifting so that she laid her head on his shoulder. It was Cat who moved his arm to wrap around her shoulders.

He sat frozen, his heart hammering. His hands tingled, and heat radiated from his chest. It took a moment for his brain to register what his body was feeling—contentment.

They sat in the darkness with nothing more than their breaths filling the silence. This time, Fintan was able to take comfort in the quiet. He closed his eyes and listened to the sounds of her breathing.

The longer she was against him, the more he relaxed and enjoyed the simplicity of the moment. He'd come to give her solace, and yet he was the one who received it.

No one had ever touched him so. Most feared him because of his reputation. That status had kept him shunned from all Fae. Others were apprehensive of him because of his looks. He'd never experienced any sort of kindness before Death found him.

He wasn't sure how to feel about his present situation. Years of witnessing humans and Fae told him that some gave affection without any deep meaning to it. Was that what this was?

The conflict within him was so great that he nearly pushed Cat away and veiled himself. The contact of her body was ... suffocating.

And wonderful.

His eyes opened as the warmth of her seeped through his clothes and into him. Her breath softly brushed against his other hand. The simple act of holding her felt so damned right.

It was as if the entire universe suddenly aligned perfectly, and he saw everything with new eyes. The world was brighter, more vivid. The air felt sweeter entering his lungs, the moonlight more brilliant as it tumbled around them.

Something fell against his hand. He looked to find a lock of her vibrant hair. He lifted the strand and twisted it around his fingers. The soft, cool texture of it was mesmerizing.

"I can't figure out what Bran wants with me."

He was startled by her whispered words. He'd thought she was asleep. "It doesn't matter."

"It does to me."

"Then we will figure it out."

She released a long breath. "I want to know how I got the dagger when I left it here."

"Does your mind ever shut off?"

"Not really."

He looked across to the opposite wall where a picture hung of a white background with an impression of gold lips. "How do you know you don't have any magic?"

"I've never been able to do anything."

"You called for your weapon. I'd say that was something."

She sat up and blinked at him. "So it was magic I used?"

"I can think of no other explanation." He reluctantly removed his arm from her, returning it to his side.

"Why can't I do it again?"

He shrugged. "You're trying too hard."

"It's frustrating."

"If you did it once, you can do it again."

She flipped her long hair over her shoulder and swallowed. "Did you have a wife before you were a Reaper?"

The question took him by surprise. He was so stunned that he could only stare. "Nay."

"Dedicated to your work?"

"Something like that."

She twisted her lips. "I had someone once, but the death of my parents was too much for him to deal with."

"Then you're better off without him."

"Yeah," she said, her brow furrowed. "I've been so worried about my grandfather and the Fae that I haven't had time to get lonely." Her head turned to him. "Is it hard for you being a Reaper and not having those relationships?"

He looked away. She was asking questions he didn't pose to

himself. Yet she was waiting for an answer, and for some reason, he didn't want to lie. "I never had any kind of relationships before I became a Reaper."

"You can't be serious."

Now uncomfortable, Fintan shrugged, wishing he'd never opened his mouth.

"You just didn't find anyone?"

He jumped up and took a few paces away before he turned to her. "No one wanted me."

For several seconds, Cat merely gawked at him with wide eyes. "I don't understand how that could be."

"It's because of who I was."

Her head tilted to the side. "Who were you?"

Damn. He really needed to stop talking. Why had he said that? Why had he allowed himself to be drawn into such a discussion? He hadn't spoken about this to anyone. Ever.

Why was he even now contemplating telling her?

"It's okay," she said. "You don't have to say any more."

Fintan inhaled deeply and released the breath. "I was born to a Dark family. The hierarchy of the Dark is much as it used to be with nobility and peasants. I came from a very poor family. They sold me as a slave to the King of the Dark, Taraeth when I was about four or five."

He heard Cat's quick intake of breath.

"I don't remember them," he told her. "I believe I had several brothers and sisters, but I can't be sure."

"You never went to look for them?"

He shot her a stern look. "Why would I want to find the family who sold me?"

"True," she mumbled.

"I probably had a better life than them anyway. I was a slave, but I never went hungry. I was clothed, fed, and had a roof over my head."

She gave him a wry look. "But you were a slave."

"A slave who had a knack for weapons and battle. Taraeth discovered when I was still just a wee lad that I was better than many of his warriors. That's when he began sending me on missions to assassinate his enemies."

Fintan didn't look at her. He couldn't. "I worked my way up in the ranks quickly because I never failed. I killed. Often. And without remorse. It didn't matter who. If my king wanted them wiped out, then I made sure it was done.

"It took eight centuries, but soon I was one of Taraeth's most trusted warriors. He gave me my freedom, but I didn't know what to do with it. When I tried to seek out friends, no one would come near me. And it wasn't just my reputation, but also my looks. I spent so many hours training and killing that I didn't know how to interact with others."

"Which is why you didn't have a wife."

He shrugged. If he were going to tell it, he might as well spill the entire story. "The only way I could have had a woman was if I paid for it, and even then, they turned their back to me during the act. A few times of that, and I decided it wasn't worth it.

"I focused everything on being the best warrior that I could. After three thousand years, I had a routine. During my slaughter of millions of Fae—Light and Dark—Taraeth was amassing power. It was Taraeth who started the civil war on our realm. I didn't know that he'd begun to feel threatened by me.

"But while he had been growing in power, so had I. My final mission for him was to kill one of his detractors, except it was a trap for me. Taraeth then handed me over to Usaeil, the Light

Queen. She tortured me for years before she grew tired and killed me."

The silence after he'd finished was thunderous. When he could stand it no more, he looked toward Cat to find her staring at him with pity in her gaze.

"Don't," he warned her angrily. "I don't want you to feel sorry for me."

She rose from the window seat and came to stand before him. Then she put her hands on either side of his face. "I'm sorry for what you suffered. It was beyond cruel."

He tried to move her hands away, but she didn't budge. Unable to help himself, he looked into her emerald eyes. Surprise rooted him in place when she rose up on her tiptoes and put her lips against his.

Then she whispered, "I want you."

He should push her away. He should return to Inchmickery. He should ... his thoughts melted away when she wrapped her arms around his neck and pressed her breasts against him.

Fintan splayed his hand on her back as he held her with his other. His eyes slid shut as their mouths brushed each other erotically. He didn't know the first thing about seduction or wooing a woman. All he knew was that he craved Cat with everything he was—and everything he wanted to be.

When their lips came together, the kiss was slow, sensual. It built quickly as the fires of desire ignited. She tasted of wildness and the sea.

And he had to have more.

He deepened the kiss, a moan tearing from him when her hands delved into his hair. Everywhere she touched left a trail of warmth, his skin tingling as if she were branding him.

Her hands moved over his chest and began to unbutton his

shirt. The first touch of her palms on his skin made him groan. She smiled against his lips and pushed the shirt over his shoulders.

He dropped his arms and let the garment fall to the floor. When he went to hold her once more, she ended the kiss and leaned back.

Since her hands were roaming over his chest, he didn't fight her. The sensations were overwhelming. No one had touched him like this. He soaked it all in, craving more, needing more.

His skin showed none of the wounds he'd received while in service to Taraeth or while Usaeil tortured him. But, somehow, Cat knew where each was because her hand would pause as if feeling the scars deep beneath his skin.

He looked down at her, completely transfixed. This was the best night of his life, and he never wanted it to end.

CHAPTER
thirteen

Cat gazed at Fintan's sculpted chest and chiseled abs. She'd felt his strength earlier, soaking it in. His smooth skin didn't have a single blemish on it, but she sensed the pain that was buried deep. Or perhaps it was her imagination after hearing about him being a slave, trained to be an assassin, and tortured.

How could anyone endure so much and still have such a good heart? It was almost inconceivable. He was a Dark. He'd killed. By his white hair and eyes, he'd killed more than any other Dark ... ever.

And yet, she knew he was good. Not only because he'd sought to help her. Because she saw it in his eyes.

She leaned close and pressed her lips over his heart. When she looked up at him, his red-rimmed, white eyes were locked on her.

Cat smiled and took a step back out of his grasp. Never taking her eyes from him, she slipped the slim straps of her gown over her shoulders and pushed it down her hips so that it puddled on the floor around her feet.

She stood still as he leisurely raked his eyes over her. His chest rumbled with a groan as her nipples hardened beneath his gaze.

It was beyond her comprehension that anyone would chose to ignore or turn away in disgust from such a man. He stirred her blood like no other. With him, the future didn't look so bleak—or lonely.

He closed the distance between them and tenderly placed his hands on her shoulders. His palms skimmed down her arms before resting on her hips. Then he moved his hands upward into the indent of her waist and then higher to her breasts.

His fingers caressed the outside of her breasts several times before lowering back down to her hips and around to her bottom.

One of his large hands cupped her butt and brought her against him. The feel of his thick arousal pressing into her stomach made her mouth go dry.

His other hand slid softly against her neck before moving around to the back. Her head dropped back. She felt his eyes on her, and her body responded shamelessly.

Her breasts ached for his touch. They swelled in anticipation when she felt his breath brush her skin. But he didn't touch her.

Instead, he brought his mouth close to her ear and said, "I want three things from you. To touch you. To taste you. To be inside you."

Chills raced over her skin at the seductive words mixed with his sexy timbre. "Yes," she said breathlessly.

In the next instant, they were lying atop her bed, and Fintan no longer wore any clothes. She widened her legs so he could settle between them, and his weight caused her sex to clench eagerly.

Her hands ran up his back, feeling the muscles beneath her palms. She couldn't stop touching him. He was perfection in every way. From the way he looked at her as if she were a goddess to how he made her feel like said goddess.

She'd never felt so beautiful or desired. The hunger, the longing was in his gaze and the way he touched her. She couldn't catch her breath. Desire encircled them, bound them. It was red-hot, causing her to feel feverish and needy.

Unable to stand it a moment longer, Cat rolled him onto his back and came up on her knees as she straddled his hips. White eyes watched her curiously, hopefully. Her heart hurt for that small bit of yearning she saw, and it made her want to seek out everyone who had dared to hurt him so she could return the favor.

She took his cock in hand and stroked up the length. He groaned loudly. Wanting him to experience as much pleasure as possible, she scooted back and bent over until her mouth was even with him.

Then she brought the thick head of his arousal to her mouth. She watched his face, noticed the way he stopped breathing. She pressed her tongue to him and parted her lips, taking him into her mouth.

He mumbled something under his breath as his head fell back, and his hands clenched the comforter. Cat inwardly smiled. She took him deep into her mouth as she continued to stroke him.

His breathing grew harsh and loud. She continued licking and sucking him before cupping his ball sac. A low groan passed his lips before he whispered her name in a voice laced with desire and need.

And it caused her stomach to clench in longing.

"I need to feel your body around me," he ground out.

She looked up at him and saw that he was barely holding onto his control. Cat gave his glorious cock one more suck before she brought him to her entrance.

His eyes burned with desire, scorched her with hunger so great, she could feel it. Slowly, she lowered herself onto his rod, taking him in inch by inch as her body stretched to accommodate him.

By the time she was fully seated, she was breathing heavily. His hands came to rest on her hips, and she slowly rotated them. His fingers dug into her. She flattened her hands on his chest and rocked back and forth.

As she rode him, his hands moved upward until he finally cupped her breasts fully. He massaged them, learning the feel before he ran a thumb over a nipple.

The pleasure that went through her was so great that she stopped moving, her breath locked in her chest. There was a smile on his lips as he rolled a nipple between his fingers.

It wasn't long before both of his fingers were teasing the tight buds. Then he sat up and wrapped his lips around one turgid peak. His tongue danced around her nipple before he suckled it.

Her arms went around his neck, her fingers into his hair as she held onto him while experiencing such heady delights. As he moved from one breast to the other, she once more began rocking her hips back and forth.

And then suddenly she was on her back, and he loomed over her. She moaned when he pulled out of her until only the head remained, and then he thrust, deeply.

Desire knotted and tightened within her, propelling her toward the pleasure that awaited. With every pump of his hips, he was pushing her closer and closer to the edge.

She wrapped her legs around him and lifted her hips to meet each of his thrusts. His rhythm quickened. Their bodies now slick with a fine sheen of sweat glided against each other sensuously.

He thrust harder, deeper. She held onto him as their wild, fiery ride bound their bodies, their souls—and their hearts.

Even as it was happening, she couldn't stop it. Nor did she want to. From the moment she'd seen Fintan, she'd known there was something different about him.

And she'd wanted him.

She looked into his eyes as she felt her orgasm building. Their gazes held as he swept her up and over the pinnacle. She cried out as her body convulsed from the force of the climax. It sent her soaring, floating in ecstasy.

A heartbeat later, he cried out her name before his orgasm claimed him. She held him as he gave a final thrust to bury himself within.

Locked in each other's arms, they soaked in the bliss of their union. They remained that way for a time. She kept touching him, caressing him. She wasn't sure if it was too much, but since he didn't pull away, she hoped it meant he enjoyed it.

"I should take you away," Fintan said as he rolled them to the side.

She actually considered it, and the relief of finally being out of danger was appealing. Then she recalled what was at stake for everyone. "We should finish what we began."

"We don't know what Bran wants with you."

"And we won't unless we stay."

He sighed loudly. "I don't like it. Any of it."

"We know he wants me for something. That's to our advantage."

"Is it?" he asked as he looked at her. "Right now, all the odds are in his favor."

She smiled at him. "Then we turn some of them our way."

"How do you propose we do that?"

"I was hoping you might know," she teased.

There was the beginning of a smile on his lips. "My plan was to lure him out into the open and kill him."

"That could still work."

"How so?"

She rose up on her elbow and smoothed his white hair away from his face. "He doesn't want to kill me. That means he'll approach me again and attempt to sway me to his side. You'll still be using me as bait, just in a different way."

"Bran will expect us to do just that."

"Then we use a different way to kill him. Instead of you, I'll do it."

Fintan sat up, shaking his head. "Absolutely not."

"He won't expect that."

"You don't know what it is to take someone's life. You don't know the toll it takes."

She raised a brow and glared at him. "Really? Did I not kill a Dark today? Isn't that essentially what Bran is, a Fae?"

"It's not the same thing," Fintan said and ran a hand down his face.

"It certainly is."

His lips flattened. "This afternoon, you were in the midst of a battle and fighting for your life. It was self-defense. If you kill Bran, it'll be murder."

"I don't consider it that. I see it as taking out a great evil that has to be stopped."

"No."

"Then come up with a different way that Bran won't suggest," she stated.

Fintan lay back and pulled her with him. "I will."

"I can do this," she said after a moment of silence.

"I know, but killing will change you. Trust me on this."

"It didn't change you inside, only your appearance."

"Not true. The darkness took me quickly and easily. I gave in to it, delighted in it. Then, one day, I didn't recognize the face staring back at me in the mirror."

She touched his long, white hair. "Because of this?"

"Because I was everything I despised. I killed so many that there isn't a shred of black in my hair anymore. Not to mention the red faded from my eyes as well. The only way I survived was by turning off every emotion I had. I buried them so deep, that they'd never come to the surface again."

That was the Fae she'd glimpsed that first night, the assassin. But the Dark before her now was someone completely different. There were emotions within him. She could see them, feel them.

"Then I met you," he said.

She touched his face, smiling.

His hand covered hers and lowered it between them. "These ... feelings ... could end up costing you your life."

"I've lived with that fear every day since my siblings were killed."

"But I'm here to protect you."

She put a finger to his lips. "Stop overthinking this. Enjoy this interlude we've gotten, because it might not come again."

The muscle tightening in his jaw told her he was doing

anything but enjoying their time together. His mind was on overload, and she couldn't imagine what he was thinking or feeling.

How long had it been since he'd buried his emotions? He hadn't turned them all off. His morality was still in place, and so was his need to protect. And there was no denying his enjoyment in killing Dark.

It was all the other emotions—desire, yearning, lust, and pleasure—he didn't know how to handle. And she could feel him shutting them down even as they lay locked in each other's arms.

fourteen

Fintan jerked upright when something passed near Cat's window. He looked outside but couldn't see anything.

"What is it?" she asked sleepily.

He swung his legs over the side of the bed and stood. With only a thought, his clothes were back in place. "I don't know."

"Wait," she called and hurried after him, tugging on a robe as she did.

Fintan didn't slow until he reached the main living area. He was about to look through the closed curtains when someone pounded on the door.

He turned to Cat, who looked at the door with a mixture of alarm and worry. She glanced his way before she headed to the entrance and looked through the peephole. "It's the Gardaí."

An Garda Síochána was the police force headed by the Garda Commissioner. Fintan should've realized they'd be by to talk to Cat about the fire at the café, as well as her grandfather's death.

"Answer it," Fintan told her. "I'll be right here, only veiled."

When she gave a nod, he concealed himself and moved to a far corner so there was no chance anyone would bump into him. Cat then took a deep breath and unlocked the door before opening it.

"Morning, Ms. Hayes," said a male voice. "I'm Detective Sergeant Carmody. I'd like to talk to you about the incidents yesterday."

Cat stepped back and allowed him inside. "Sure."

Fintan watched as a man in his late forties walked into the house. Carmody's gaze moved around, taking everything in. Fintan stared at the Sergeant with his blond hair and dark eyes trying to determine if it was Bran using glamour, but Fintan could find nothing. That didn't mean Bran wasn't responsible for sending the man.

Or was Fintan looking for things that weren't there?

Before he met Cat, he would've had no problem determining if Carmody were connected to Bran. Now, he couldn't see through the fog of emotions that filled his brain.

And he hated it.

"Can I get you a cup of tea?" Cat asked.

The Sergeant gave a shake of his head. "No, thanks."

"Please sit," she said as she tucked a leg and took one corner of the sofa.

Carmody chose a chair and gave her a polite—if forced—smile. "I'm sorry about the loss of your grandfather. I know you're grieving, but I must ask you some questions."

"Of course." Cat clasped her hands in her lap and kept her gaze on the Sergeant.

Her shoulders were tense, and Fintan had the insane urge to touch her to let her know he was there. But he held himself in check.

What is fekking wrong with me?

"Ms. Hayes, where were you when the café fire began?" Carmody asked as he took out a small notebook and a pen.

She swallowed and said in a clear voice, "Right here in my house. I'm sure if you check with the owner of the shop next to my café, Norene, she'll confirm that she called me. I'm also sure you can check the mobile phone records, which will show my location."

"You act as if you have something to hide."

"I'm merely pointing out the facts to hurry along this process. The café is my livelihood. Without it, I can't pay my bills. So until the investigation is closed, my insurance won't pay out so I can fix what happened."

"Do you know how the fire began?" he asked.

Fintan moved closer and watched the Garda carefully as he jotted down notes—some relevant to his questioning, and some comments to himself about her answers.

Carmody wasn't accusing Cat, but there was something in the man's dark eyes as he watched her, that set Fintan off.

"A fire burned down my café," Cat stated. "I don't know how it started."

"We're investigating that now. We should know something in a few weeks."

She gave a shake of her head, anger spiking her voice. "A few weeks? You can't be serious."

"These things take time, Ms. Hayes."

"It took the Garda office three days to rule on a business fire last year."

Carmody's lips twisted as he shrugged. "I don't make the rules, miss. Do you know anyone who would want to harm you?"

"No," Cat said and blew out a breath. She braced her elbow on the arm of the sofa and propped her fist against her temple.

Fintan frowned when he saw the word frustrated was circled several times. There was a question mark beside the word innocent.

But it was the knowledgeable about phone tracing with an asterisk next to it that caused a spike of fury to flash through Fintan. How dare Carmody think Cat manipulated events to suit her purpose?

Carmody coughed softly. "Did you set the fire to claim the insurance money?"

For long seconds, Cat merely stared at him. Then she got to her feet with irritation flaring in the emerald depths of her eyes. "No. Would you like to look at my books to make sure I was in the black? I'll be happy to hand them over to prove my innocence if it will take me off your suspect list."

"Ms. Hayes, you need to understand that it wasn't just the fire at the café. Your grandfather's body was burned, as well. There's a connection there, and I aim to find it."

Fintan knew the correlation: Bran. But it wasn't as if Cat could tell the Garda that. Which left her looking like the prime suspect.

"I know full well what occurred with my grandfather. I'm the one who saw the smoke and went to him."

"With what?" Carmody asked. "Your vehicle was parked in the driveway."

Fintan fisted his hand. That was his fault. He was the one who'd teleported Cat to the beach. If only he'd have thought things through, he would've known she needed her car. But he'd only wanted to help her. So he'd acted rashly.

That never happened.

Now, his thoughtlessness might very well ruin things for her.

"I'd needed to walk to clear my head after the café fire," Cat said. "I headed to his cottage. Halfway there, I saw the smoke and ran the rest of the way. Of course, I didn't have my car."

Carmody nodded. "What did you find when you reached your grandfather's?"

"I already went over this yesterday," she stated irritably.

"I need you to do it again."

While Fintan listened to Cat explain finding the shed burning and then discovering her grandfather inside, he watched Carmody. It was clear that the Garda didn't exactly believe Cat was a victim, but Carmody didn't have any evidence to prove otherwise.

"That matches your statement from yesterday," Carmody said as he stood. "That's all I need."

While Cat walked him to the door, Fintan looked through the slit in the curtains and spotted a Fae watching the house. The Dark had used glamour to alter her hair and eyes. When Carmody exited the house, the Dark vanished.

"He thinks I did it," Cat said as she shut and locked the door.

Fintan dropped the veil. "With both events happening within hours of each other and both connected to you, it only seems natural. Yet there is no evidence against you."

"That we know of," she said crossly. "For all we know, Bran is planting evidence now."

He followed her to the bedroom. "If Bran wants you on his side, I doubt he'd take the time to put you in the crosshairs of the Garda."

"Why not? Then he could get me out. That's what I'd do," she said and peeled off the robe.

The sight of her naked body made his balls tighten. Her pale skin and pink nipples had him aching to be inside her once more, to feel the profound and exquisite pleasure she'd shown him.

In one night, he'd experienced more bliss than the whole of his life. She'd freely and willingly touched him, caressed him. Learned him. She'd given herself to him. And in doing so, she'd shown him sensual decadence that was now branded upon his soul.

She strode past him, seemingly indifferent to his gaze feasting on her gorgeous flesh, and headed for the bathroom.

His eyes dropped to her bottom, watching her hips sway with each step. He remembered the feel of those hips moving as she sat atop him and brought him into her body.

"By your silence, you agree."

He blinked, his mind pulled back to the present. "I agree that it could be a ploy, but I don't think Bran would go that route when there's another way."

She turned the shower on. "What might that be?"

"Coming to you himself." He walked to the bathroom doorway and leaned a shoulder against the jamb as he watched her testing the water.

"You really think he's going to just come up to me?" she asked with a laugh.

He crossed his arms over his chest. "I would."

She looked at him over her shoulder before wrinkling her nose. "I suppose. But won't he realize you're with me?"

"I'm sure he's counting on it."

Cat pinned her hair atop her head and climbed into the bathtub before she pulled the clear shower curtain closed. "Bran is nuts if he thinks I'll go anywhere with him if he attempts to kill you."

"I'm glad to hear it." He was trying—and failing—not to look at her and think of the water gliding over the skin he'd touched and kissed just hours earlier.

He tried not to think of her ragged breaths, her moans of pleasure, and her cries of ecstasy. The more he attempted to turn his mind away from it, the more the entire night replayed in his head.

His gaze followed her movements as she soaped up her body then rinsed off. He'd never seen anything so sexy. The fact that no Fae female would ever let him this close was partly to blame for his fascination.

"Please tell me you don't want me to sit around waiting for Bran to pop into my kitchen," she said as she turned off the water. She pushed the shower curtain open and held out her hand.

Fintan handed her a towel. "Bran can't get inside the house anymore. I warded it."

A slim red brow lifted. "Is that so?"

"You need to be safe somewhere."

"And how are you still inside, then?"

He smiled. "I'm that good."

"Yes. I know you are."

Her seductive look had him hard in an instant. She smiled as if knowing what she'd done. Then she stepped out of the tub and hung up the towel.

When she walked out of the bathroom, he sighed. How was he ever supposed to think straight when she looked at him in that way after making such a comment with carnal undertones?

He walked into the living room and thought of Bran. What was the bastard's next move? Bran wanted Cat, but why had he killed the grandfather? Something didn't make sense. There was a piece missing, some knowledge Fintan lacked that could help him see the bigger picture.

"Staring at the wall isn't going to give us answers," Cat said as she came up beside him. "We need more information."

He hated that clothes now covered her amazing body. "And by that, you mean finding Bran."

"Where else but with him will we find out what we need to know?"

Fintan shook his head. "Cat, you're playing a dangerous game. You've not seen what Bran can do. He manipulates people and things to his advantage. You can't believe anything he tells you."

"I won't. But you know I'm right. We need information."

No matter how he looked at it, he couldn't make a move without knowing more about Bran's interest in Cat.

And how she had called the weapon.

CHAPTER

Cat walked from Galway through the paths toward her grandfather's cottage with a mist of rain being blown about by the high winds. But it wasn't the weather that concerned her.

Though it had been her idea to be somewhere Bran could reach her, she'd been more confident in her own home. It didn't matter that Fintan was veiled behind her. For all intents and purposes, she was alone.

And that scared her.

She put her hands in her coat pockets and huddled in the scarf she'd wrapped around her neck. The ice in her veins from fear only made her colder.

With each step that took her away from Galway, she knew something big was going to happen. She didn't know what or how, but it was a sensation she couldn't shake.

She blinked against the wind that cut into her eyes, already itchy from lack of sleep. It had been dreams of her grandfather dying that had kept waking her. Though, each time, Fintan was there with his arms around her. It was his presence that had allowed her to drift back off.

In between the few hours of rest she'd gotten, she thought about the dagger—the same weapon that was now hidden in her jacket.

There was no explanation for how the blade had gone from her kitchen table to her hand. Fintan couldn't give her an answer, but maybe Bran could. That is if she wanted him to know she had that ability.

Ha. Ability. She rolled her eyes. She, more than anyone, knew that she had no magic. Nothing she'd done growing up had produced even a thimbleful of it. So, why now?

Was it the weapon?

No, that couldn't be it. If it were, Fintan would've told her.

Was it Fintan?

He was a Reaper, but he hadn't mentioned any of the other Halflings suddenly finding magic with the Reapers around. So that was out.

Was it Bran?

This one stumped her because she honestly didn't know. She couldn't come up with a reason to exclude him as she had the other things. But at the same time, she couldn't say it was him, either. It was a conundrum.

Her steps slowed when the cottage came into sight. She hadn't been able to look at it yesterday—the grief had been too raw. And today wasn't much better.

She was alone. Completely alone now. Holidays wouldn't be spent surrounded by family with laughter and stories from prior years. They would now be spent in the quiet of her house, pretending that whatever holiday it was didn't exist.

God, how she hated the Fae. Why couldn't they have left her family alone? Why had she been born a Halfling? Why couldn't she have had a normal family that fought all the time? At least they'd be alive.

A family that hounded her about her poor decisions or her hair or a man. A family who would call, demanding that she come for Sunday dinner every week, or who popped by without calling. A family who made her drink excessively at Christmas because being surrounded by all of them gave her hives.

Any family at all would be welcome. No matter the problems, no matter how much they might drive her mad, she just wanted family again.

The loneliness had never struck her so hard as it did at that moment. It cut through her, causing her to gasp from the pain of it.

She made her way to the burnt shed where she'd seen Bran beckoning her. Fintan was sure he was watching her. She hoped Bran was because she was ready to talk. Though she wasn't sure if she was all that ready to hear what he might say.

That's what made her stomach clench in dread. A gnawing, churning feeling in her gut that had begun the moment she'd gotten out of bed that morning. It was a sensation that something was about to happen, and she had a suspicion that it wasn't going to be very good.

The thing was, if Fintan knew Bran was watching, then Bran had to know Fintan would be veiled and waiting near her. Fintan was only one Reaper, and Bran would have other men with him.

Which meant there was a very good chance Bran would kill Fintan. That couldn't happen. She refused to allow such a thing to occur.

She might not have been able to save anyone in her family, but there was a tiny, infinitesimal chance that she could keep Fintan safe. After everything he'd done for her—was still doing—she had to try.

It wasn't just keeping Fintan alive. There was also a burning need to know what Bran wanted with her.

She squeezed her tired eyes shut. If only she could be somewhere where Bran couldn't hurt her but that Fintan couldn't see them. Thereby allowing her to get all the information she needed.

When she opened her eyes, Bran stood in front of her.

She was so startled that she took a step back. For his part, Bran merely looked pleased.

"Hello, Cat," he said. "I knew it was only a matter of time before you and I were able to talk." His silver eyes held no malice, but then again, madmen often hid their true feelings.

"Here I am. Talk." She sounded much braver than she felt. Was Fintan near enough to hear the conversation?

"Don't you want to know about me?"

"I already do," she retorted. It took every ounce of willpower not to look around for Fintan.

Bran scrutinized her curiously and smiled. "Well, that's not quite fair, now is it? Considering you heard my story from a third party who wasn't even there."

"There were rules, you broke them, Death killed your woman, you got angry and divided the Reapers, and then you killed some. All before Death put you in the Netherworld. Did I leave anything out?"

Instead of becoming angry, Bran threw back his head and laughed. "Oh, you are a treasure, Catriona Hayes. Now I wish we would've talked much sooner."

"Because I say what I want?" she asked sarcastically.

"Yes."

She wasn't fooled by his charm or the fact that his eyes were silver instead of the red they should be. "Is there anything you want to add to the story about you?"

The smile melted from his face as his gaze became haunted. It was there just a moment before the look was shuttered and replaced with a mask of indifference. "Have you ever been in love?"

"I can't say that I have."

"Then you don't know what it means to find someone who is your other half, who fills a void you didn't know you had until you met them."

Her thoughts immediately turned to Fintan. Was it Fate that put a Fae in her path, one who gave her all those things? "I don't, no."

"What a pity. Maybe then you would understand the depth of my anguish when Death killed her."

"You broke the rules. What did you expect?"

"I expected that my time and loyalty to the Reapers would earn me some leniency." Bran snorted and looked over her shoulder toward the sea. "Instead, the love of my life was killed before I could warn her or say good-bye."

There was a part of Cat that began to feel sorry for him until she recalled what he'd done next in the story. "That still doesn't give you the right to break the rules and expect special treatment. Nor does it give you leave to kill your brethren."

"Death's time is setting. Mine is rising. It's why she didn't want any of us to love."

Cat raised a brow at the use of she. So Death was a female. She hadn't seen that one coming. But she quite liked the idea. "You believe that Death put the rule that you couldn't have a relationship in place because it would give you more power if you had someone to love?"

"I do."

"Then why are there three Reapers who have fallen in love and brought their women into the fold?"

Bran's face didn't change, but the force of his fury nearly bowled her over. "What did you say?"

Shit. Was she not supposed to tell him that? Was it a secret the Reapers were keeping? If only she would've thought to ask Fintan.

"Tell me," Bran demanded.

She immediately took offense and put a hand up to keep him away. "I don't have to tell you a damn thing."

He began to take a step toward her, then thought better of it. "You're right. You don't. It's your choice."

"What do you want with me?" It was time to change the subject—and get some answers.

Bran looked at her curiously. "It really isn't an act, is it?"

"What? That I have no magic? Of course, it's not an act."

His lips lifted in a smile. "Who lied to you, Cat?"

"No one lied to me. I've known my entire life."

"That's not true."

She frowned at him, hating the spike of hope that surged within her. "What do you mean?"

"How did you call the weapon yesterday?"

"I don't know."

He nodded slowly, his lips twisting as he gazed at her. "And how did you call me?"

"I don't have any idea what you're talking about."

"Look around, my dear girl."

Cat was suddenly afraid to. That knot in her stomach twisted painfully. She took a deep breath and then turned. Her mouth fell open when she saw that there was a clear dome around them.

"What did you say or think about me?" Bran urged.

"That I wanted to talk somewhere you couldn't harm me." She left off the thought about Fintan. No need to alert Bran that he was near.

Bran laughed. "Brilliant. Perfectly brilliant."

She turned back to face him. "You're saying I did this?"

"Of course."

"How? How is this possible when I've not been able to do anything magical before?" she asked.

His smile was sly, cunning, and it instantly put her on edge and had warning bells tolling in her head.

Bran held out his hand. "Come with me, and I'll tell you everything."

"No."

He lifted his brows. "You might want to rethink that."

"The answer is a firm, and final, no," she declared.

His arm dropped to his side as he tsked. "What a pity. I thought you might want to see your grandfather."

Of all the things she'd thought he might say, that had never occurred to her. With the grief still so fresh and raw, her fury went through the roof.

"How dare you," she said with every ounce of her fury lacing her words. "How fekking dare you. Who do you think you are to play with someone's emotions like that? I'm going to make sure you go back to the Netherworld because I'm going to take your sorry ass there myself."

She yanked the dagger from her jacket and launched herself at Bran. He fell back on the sand, not bothering to defend himself.

She didn't care. All she knew was that the one responsible for her grandfather's death was right before her.

And it was time for payback.

She sliced his chest once, twice. Then she raised the weapon over her head to plunge it into his heart. That's when she saw his arms out at his sides, his eyes staring at her without an ounce of fear.

"Why aren't you defending yourself?" she demanded.

He shrugged helplessly. "I can't. It's your magic."

"So I could kill you now."

"Yes."

"Good," she said and raised the weapon higher.

His eyes widened, a hint of fear showing. "Wait! Don't you want to know about your grandfather?"

"You're lying about him."

"Am I?"

The taunt was there, hanging between them. Fintan told her not to believe anything Bran said. Then there was the part where she could end the war Fintan and the other Reapers were involved in.

But what if Bran were telling the truth? What if he had her grandfather?

"Whose body burned?" she asked.

Bran lifted his shoulders. "I told Searlas to find a mortal."

Cat lowered the weapon. She couldn't believe she wasn't going to kill him, but the thought of possibly having her grandfather returned was too good to pass up.

She got off Bran and stood. "If you're right and I can use magic for things like this," she said, waving her hands at the dome, "then I can do it again and kill you."

"If that's what you believe."

There was something about his words that bothered her. "I want proof that my grandfather is still alive. Once I have it, then we'll talk."

"That's a reasonable enough deal. However, you're going to have to rid yourself of a Reaper."

"Go away," she told him, wishing it with all her might.

And he did.

The dome vanished, as well, and in the next heartbeat, Fintan stood before her with rage shining in his red-rimmed white eyes.

CHAPTER
sixteen

The wariness in Fintan's eyes caused Cat to second-guess her decision. He might not have been able to see her with Bran, but he knew. It was there in his gaze, in the condemning way he looked at her.

She didn't step back, though she wanted to. She stood her ground, chin up.

"What did you do?" he demanded.

An avalanche of words tumbled through her mind, but there wasn't a single one she found that could be used to make him understand why she'd done what she'd done.

"Cat," he said. "Tell me what you did."

It didn't matter if she wanted to tell him or not because she knew she couldn't. What had happened with Bran needed to be kept from Fintan. For now.

At least, until she knew if Bran spoke the truth about her grandfather or not.

But there was one thing she could tell him.

"I used magic."

There was no surprise on his face, no form of delight at the news. Instead, he stood stoic and apathetic. "Magic."

"Yes."

"For someone who has stated many times she wasn't able to use magic, you now suddenly have it. Strange, is it not?"

She swallowed, hating the gulf that divided them. She reached out her hand, grasping his arm. Last night, she'd never felt closer to another person. And now ... she'd never felt farther away.

"I didn't lie to you before. I honestly believed I didn't have any. The more I thought about the dagger, the more I wanted to replicate what I did. So I tried."

"How?" he demanded.

She couldn't tell him about Bran. Not even when there was a chance he might understand because of her grandfather. Simply because she knew Fintan would come to one conclusion: that she had betrayed him.

She'd cornered Bran, but she hadn't allowed Fintan near to kill Bran and end the war. He'd be furious.

And rightly so.

Yet, he'd given her nothing but honesty since coming into her life. How could she not give him at least the same?

"When the dagger came to me, I'd been thinking about it. That's what I did this time."

His white eyes narrowed a fraction. "Just what did you think about?"

"Wanting to be hidden." It wasn't a complete lie.

It also wasn't the entire truth. Which, ultimately, was a lie.

And she felt like a piece of shite.

If it were possible, Fintan's rage elevated several levels. He didn't move, didn't utter a single word. But it was there in the way he stood, tense and rigid. It was there in the way he stared at her as if she were a stranger—as if she couldn't be trusted.

She fought the tears that threatened, blinking rapidly. She would not cry for what she had destroyed. She would not. Because it was for her grandfather.

Fintan was a wonderful Fae with an amazing body, but he was so broken, she wasn't sure anyone could ever mend him—if he even wanted to be healed.

But in the end, she had to think of her future. The smallest thread of hope that her grandfather could be alive was too great to pass up.

Even if her heart hurt at the idea of losing Fintan.

Regardless, she hadn't committed to Bran. If she learned the body at the morgue was indeed her grandfather, or if Bran couldn't give her proof of life, then she would tell Fintan everything.

Even though it would destroy what little trust he had in her. Surely, he would understand.

She didn't want to think about what would happen if she learned her grandfather was alive and well. Because whatever Bran wanted couldn't be good. She would, in fact, possibly be betraying Fintan and the other Reapers.

Without a word, Fintan veiled himself. At least she assumed he did. For all she knew, he could've teleported away. And she couldn't blame him.

He knew she wasn't telling him everything. Instead of demanding she share what she hid, he'd let the half-truth hang between them.

She looked down at her hands. If she had called the dagger, and if she had brought Bran to her and created the dome, why couldn't she feel the magic?

Domhnall and Nora had often spoken of how it felt to feel their magic. She even recalled her father and grandfather speaking of it.

Cat dropped her arms to her sides and turned toward the cottage. She walked to it, pausing briefly at the door before continuing inside. Her gaze searched everything, looking for any sign of a struggle or anything that would give her a clue that he was alive.

Everything was as orderly and clean as always. The kettle set on the stove. A cup had been washed and left upside down on a towel next to the sink to dry. A book waited on the table with a clip marking over half the story read.

It looked as if her grandfather had just taken a walk on the beach and would return shortly. She grasped the hope tightly that he was alive.

"Cat, a stóirín."

She closed her eyes at the sound of her grandfather's voice behind her. It could all be a trick. Or he might be the real thing.

Slowly, she turned and opened her eyes. She gazed into the weathered face she knew so well. Her heart was so overjoyed she thought it might burst from her chest.

She ran to him, throwing her arms around his neck, only to be met with air. She looked at her empty arms and spun around to look for him.

Her grandfather's face was filled with sadness and regret. "This is as close as he'll allow me to get to you."

"Who?" she asked, but she knew the answer.

"Bran."

"What does he want with you?"

Her grandfather shook his head. "Ah, girl. It's you he wants."

"Why?"

"Because of the power within you."

She gawked at him, stunned to her bones. "You say that as if you know I have magic."

"I've always known. So did your parents. We were protecting you."

"From what?" she cried.

The deception of her family was a swift and cruel blow. All those years she'd cried herself to sleep because she was without magic. All those years she'd felt inferior. All the time she'd felt excluded.

And they'd known the truth.

Her grandfather raised his hands before him. "Listen. We don't have much time. Save your anger."

Save it? Was he serious? She was going to unleash it on someone. Namely Bran.

"Your magic manifested itself when you were just a wee babe. It grew out of control so quickly that I had no choice but to step in when your father couldn't control it," he said.

She fisted her hands in an effort not to lash out at her grandfather. "What are you talking about?"

"All you have to do is think of something, a stóirín, and it's yours."

"You can't be serious."

Bushy white eyebrows rose in his forehead. "What have you thought about recently and suddenly had, unsure of how it came to be?"

Her mind immediately went to the dagger. Then there was Fintan. Last night, she'd wished he were with her so she wouldn't have to be alone, and he'd walked into her room. Then there was Bran just a bit ago, along with the dome.

"By your face, there are several instances." Her grandfather released a long sigh. "When Bran took me away, it severed my connection with you, which broke the spell I'd used to bind your magic. You have precious little time to learn to control your thoughts so your magic doesn't manifest into reality."

She put her hand to her forehead. "This can't be happening."

"I'm sorry, but it is."

"Why haven't you told me until now?"" she demanded.

He glanced at the floor. "Three Fae, Cat. Three. No other Halfling family in the world has had more than one Fae beget a child. We have targets on our backs because of this, my girl."

"That still doesn't explain why you've kept the truth from me all these years?"

"I wanted to protect you."

She threw up her hands in agitation. "Why?" she demanded again.

"Because you're ... different. I knew it as soon as you were born."

She didn't want to be angry with her grandfather, but there was no controlling it. "You could've told me. I could've been working all these years to control this."

"It doesn't work that way. Your magic is like a magnet to the Fae."

This only confused her more. "Why?"

"All the magic in all the generations of our family has culminated in you, a stóirín. I don't know how or why, but that's the truth of it. It's why I bound your magic. You see, you have great power within you. It's so formidable that you can be used to do good or evil. The choice is yours."

Her arm fell to her side as her stomach revolted at his words. She walked to the table and pulled out one of the chairs before she dropped down on it. "Bran killed Domhnall and Nora."

"I know. He gloated over the fact."

"Bran wants to kill Death and the Reapers," she said, looking up at her grandfather, who had come to stand beside the table.

He gave a shake of his head. "Death? Reapers? I heard stories when I was a lad, but I never expected them to be real."

"They are. Death put Bran in a prison realm called the Netherworld because he broke her rules then killed two of his fellow Reapers."

Her grandfather's eyes widened. "If that's true, you cannot give him anything, no matter what he uses against you."

"If I don't go to him, he won't release you."

"He won't ever release me," he said with a sad smile. "Bran will use me to get you to do whatever he wants. I'm an old man. I've lived my life. Forget me and go live yours. Do good with your magic. Continue the legacy of our family."

He made it sound so easy, but it wasn't. She'd never be able to live with herself if he died because she didn't help. Then again, she'd never be able to live with herself if Bran won against the Reapers and Fintan was killed.

Either way, she was going to lose.

"Cat," her grandfather called.

She saw him begin to fade away. "No," she cried, jumping to her feet, her arm outstretched, reaching for him.

But her grandfather was already gone.

Once more alone in the cottage, she dropped to her knees and buried her face in her hands. The torrent of tears came, choking her.

She threw back her head, screaming her anguish, anger, and frustration. She shouted until her throat hurt, and then she yelled some more.

But it did nothing to ease her troubled soul.

Her mind went to Fintan. How she wished he were there, his

strong arms around her. He would know what to do. He always did. If he could forgive her.

More tears gathered in her eyes, spilling down her cheeks. She was in a tricky spot, and there was no way she could come out a winner.

It didn't seem fair to finally discover that she had magic and learn why it had been concealed, only to find that it was her magic that had brought the worst kind of evil to her door.

And the best of men, as well.

If only she'd told Fintan everything from the beginning. But she knew he would advise her to do the very thing her grandfather had.

Two men she trusted and regarded highly had the same opinion, but she couldn't let go of the fact that she wouldn't be alone if she did what Bran wanted. She would have her grandfather.

Her head jerked up as she blinked through the tears. Her grandfather had said she could get whatever she wanted just by thinking about it. So she thought about him, of wanting him there beside her without any restrictions from Bran.

Yet nothing happened.

She tried again and again and again, exhausting herself in the process. It took a toll on her body, sapping her of all strength so that her arms couldn't hold her up. Lying half on her stomach, half on her side, she cried for all that was, all that could've been.

And all that would never be.

It was hours later that she had to concede that Bran had put something in place to prevent her from using her magic on her grandfather. And the realization was too much for her to take.

Anger gave her a flood of energy, enough that she was able to push herself up onto all fours. Then, using every last bit of strength she had, Cat grasped anything she could to help her get to her feet.

Once there, she swayed, but she was determined not to fall. She put one foot in front of the other and made her way to the door. Opening it, she looked outside. The rain came down faster as the wind caused it to fall at an angle. The walk home was going to get her drenched.

She looked over her shoulder at the cottage, briefly contemplating remaining there, but she couldn't. Because Fintan wouldn't be able to come to her. And right now, she needed him.

There was a part of her that wanted to wish for him, but forcing him to come to her didn't seem right after lying to him. Even if she needed him so badly that she thought she might die without him.

How she wished she were in her own home. The thought barely went through her head when she found herself standing in the middle of her living room. She turned in a circle, shocked at what had just happened.

"Fintan," she called and rushed from room to room, looking for him. "Fintan!"

But it didn't matter how many times she called for him, he didn't appear. She knew he could hear her. It was his choice to stay away. Though she had a way to bring him to her, she didn't use it.

If he didn't want to be with her, she wouldn't make him. She'd hurt him deeply, and he might never forgive her for that.

She removed her scarf and coat and hung them up. It had been a day of emotions that brought her high, and ones that dragged her so low she wondered if she could ever get up again.

The absolute worst was knowing that her actions had sent Fintan away.

Possibly for good.

CHAPTER
seventeen

Fintan knew the taste of betrayal all too well. The fact that it lingered on his tongue yet again left him grim and miserable. It was a wretched thing indeed to give someone trust, only to have it snatched away so quickly.

Despite his feelings, he didn't abandon Cat. He continued to watch over her. Even when she was inside the beach cottage, he'd observed her through the window.

It didn't take a great mind to sort out what was happening. Fintan was angry with himself for not realizing it sooner. Bran's ploy was so basic, so ironclad that it had been easy to look for something bigger and more dramatic.

The simple fact was that Bran had Cat's grandfather. It was the clear and only way Bran would ever coax her to his side. Knowing why she lied didn't make it hurt any less, though. It meant that Cat didn't trust him enough to help.

And she was right. He wouldn't. He'd talk her out of anything to do with Bran. He'd tell her to look at the big picture, to think of the fate of the world versus one man who was in the golden years of his life.

Fintan would wear her down until she agreed. The Reapers would triumph over Bran, and the war he'd begun would end. Things would go back to normal.

While Cat was left alone to deal with what she'd done. Hate would enter her heart and be directed towards him, and she'd never forgive him.

There would be no happy ending for him either. Their night of passion, a night that had changed him, would crumble into nothing.

But the feelings would still be there. He'd still long for her. It would be that yearning that reminded him of what he'd done. Of what he lost.

That guilt would build over the centuries until he began to hate himself. That disgust would eat him from the inside out until his brothers had no choice but to kill him.

All because Bran had escaped the Netherworld and sought revenge.

It didn't matter how he looked at it, Fintan couldn't find a solution. By the way Cat had lied to him, she'd already made her decision to go with Bran. And he couldn't blame her.

She remembered her family. She knew what it was to be a part of a group who loved unconditionally. She'd watched each of them be taken from her, leaving her completely alone.

He recalled nothing of his family. Not how many siblings he'd had, or even a hint of what either of his parents' faces looked like. He'd been abandoned. All he'd ever known was loneliness. Cat had a chance to change that. In her shoes, he'd do the same.

His thoughts ground to a halt as he reflected on Eoghan. How was it that he'd never thought of the Reapers as his family? It wasn't until now, at that moment, that Fintan realized that's exactly who they were.

He called them his brothers, but he'd kept himself distant from them—just in case. All that changed with Bran. Fintan had subconsciously—or perhaps he'd knowingly done it—bonded with the Reapers.

Eoghan's disappearance haunted him. Fintan wanted to find Eoghan, needed to find him. It's what drove him to hurry and kill Bran so that the Reapers could put their focus where it needed to be—Eoghan.

All this time, he'd just thought he was part of a group. He was always on the fringes, always watching Kyran and Talin joke with each other while Cael sought patience. Baylon would egg things on, and Eoghan would stand guard in muted silence.

Fintan looked across the street to Cat's house. The curtains were open, but he didn't approach. Her magic had brought her there. He hadn't seen any movement, but he didn't expect Bran or any of his men to get anywhere near her.

In some ways, Cat was safer now than she had been. What Fintan wanted to know was how Bran had discovered her? How had he known she had magic?

It was her power that stumped Fintan. A Fae could think of something and have it appear or disappear. He did it with his sword all the time. The same with the teleportation.

The fact that she, as a Halfling, was exhibiting the same type of magic as a Fae was interesting. The Fae often put spells on their children to keep them close until they grew old enough to learn to control it. And Fintan suspected that's exactly what Cat's grandfather had done.

None of that explained why Bran wanted her, though. If her magic was much like a Fae's, then he could grab anyone and get what he wanted. It had to be something singular about Cat. Something that only she could do.

Since Fintan had never paid much attention to Halflings, he was at a loss. It could be anything. The scope of possibilities that sat before him was endless.

There was one person who would know. Yet Fintan wasn't at all eager to have an audience with Death. It didn't matter that he'd seen her more times over the last few weeks than the last several millennia. Death was ... Death. She held more power and magic in her little finger than all the Fae combined.

The sight of long, black and silver hair out of the corner of his eye caught Fintan's attention. He turned his head and stared in surprise at Balladyn.

Fintan used glamour to hide his hair and eyes before he dropped the veil. Balladyn's head turned toward him immediately. The Dark stared for a moment, then made his way to Fintan.

Balladyn was once the Captain of the Queen's Guard and a famed warrior in the Light army until he ended up wounded and in the hands of the Dark after a battle.

There was much Balladyn was unaware of. Especially the part about how his own queen, Usaeil, had betrayed him and handed him over to the Dark.

Fintan didn't feel inclined to open the Dark's eyes. Mostly because Balladyn was now the Dark King's right hand. While Taraeth had assumed that Fintan wanted to take over and had him killed because of it, the king seemed oblivious to the fact that Balladyn might very well do the deed.

"Who are you?" Balladyn asked as he approached.

Fintan shrugged. "Nobody."

"You're using glamour. Why?"

"For obvious reasons."

Balladyn's red eyes looked him up and down. "You don't want me to see who you really are. Are you Light?"

"Do you think I'll give you an honest answer?"

The Dark smiled, approval in his eyes. "No."

"What is Taraeth's lieutenant doing walking the streets of Galway?" Fintan asked.

"No reason."

So, neither was going to give anything away. Perhaps Fintan had been wrong to think Balladyn might know something. It had been an impulsive move to show himself to the Dark, and impulsive Fintan was not.

Just another way Cat had changed him.

"You look like you have something on your mind," Balladyn said.

Fintan held back a snort. "You could say that."

"Does it have anything to do with the Halfling across the street?"

"You know Catriona Hayes?" Fintan asked, surprised.

Balladyn nodded and moved into the alley with Fintan. "A Fae can't be in this city without knowing of her and the Hayes family."

"I only recently learned about her. What do you know?"

The Dark stared at him for a long moment. "Do you want to be the fourth Fae who leaves a child with the family?"

The impact of Balladyn's words hit Fintan with the all the gentleness of a tsunami. A child. A child? There was certainly a possibility since he hadn't thought about anything other than being inside Cat's body while they were making love.

He was the last person—or Fae—in any realm who would make a good father. He barely knew how to be a friend. He knew nothing of lovers, and even less about being a parent.

"Easy there," Balladyn said with a chuckle. "You've gone pale."

Fintan inwardly shook himself. "I don't want children."

"You and me both, my friend. So why are you curious about Catriona?"

"I want to know why every Fae around watches her."

Balladyn crossed his arms over his chest and turned his red eyes to Cat's house. "I think most try to see if they'll be here when she's killed. It's odd that across the realm, Halflings have been murdered left and right. There are Fae who say it's the Reapers' doing."

"You sound like you don't believe that."

"I don't." Balladyn cut his eyes to him and shrugged. "Or maybe it is. Who knows?"

Interesting. First Fintan had seen that Balladyn wasn't helping Taraeth, and now the Dark had a different opinion about the Reapers than other Fae.

Balladyn continued talking. "The fact is that Catriona doesn't fit in our world or her own. Have you seen how the mortals treat her? They know she's different. They keep their distance. They're polite, but that's as far as it goes."

He had been too wrapped up with trying to catch Bran, find Eoghan, and get Cat on his side to notice such things. When he looked toward the house again, he saw Cat standing in the kitchen, chopping garlic as she prepared to cook.

"Do you feel sorry for her?" Fintan asked.

Balladyn lifted one shoulder. "As a Light, I would've said yes. As a Dark, I don't really care. So tell me, how do you know who I am?"

"Everyone knows you," Fintan said and met Balladyn's gaze.

"I don't sense any fear in you. Most fear me."

"The only thing I fear is Death."

Balladyn laughed. "Everyone fears death."

Fintan let him think he was talking about the act and not the person. "Your position within the king's court must give you access to a lot of people."

"Aye." He turned to face Fintan then. "What is it you're looking for?"

"Information."

Balladyn cocked his head to the side. "I'm not in the habit of just giving away such things for free."

"What do you want in exchange?"

"I want to see you. Drop the glamour."

Fintan hesitated. It had been a long time since he'd been in Taraeth's court. So long, in fact, that few would remember him. But his coloring made him extremely memorable. And he didn't want to be remembered.

"So, you do fear me," Balladyn said with a sly grin. "Otherwise, what do you have to hide?"

Fintan dropped the glamour. He watched as Balladyn's smile dropped and a frown formed. Fintan was used to people ogling him, and for the most part, he didn't care. But it was the manner in which the Dark was staring—as if he recognized him.

"I have an affinity for books," Balladyn said. "I collect any and all. Once, long ago, I read about a white-haired Dark who was the most deadly assassin the Fae had ever encountered."

Fintan was shocked. Had someone actually written about him? He wasn't sure how to respond to such a statement. "What happened to him?"

"No one knows," Balladyn said. "Some believe he's still very much alive. Others think he went away. Still others believe Taraeth betrayed him to Usaeil, who ultimately killed him. Which is it?"

"All of them. None of them. You asked me to reveal myself. I did. You said nothing about wanting to know my story."

"Something I regret greatly." Balladyn blew out a breath and dropped his arms to his sides. "I promised you information. What is it you want?"

Fintan glanced at Cat once more. "Do you have Dark disappearing?"

Balladyn's gaze intensified. "Yes. We can't figure out where."

"Do you know anything about a Fae named Bran?"

"Unfortunately not. Is he responsible for the Dark vanishing?"

If Fintan gave this information, he wouldn't be revealing anything about the Reapers. Not directly. In fact, Balladyn might very well be able to help in the capture of Bran. Fintan would love to return to the Reapers' holding in Inchmickery with the news that Bran was dead.

"Yes."

Balladyn smiled. "Tell me more."

CHAPTER eighteen

The chiming of the clock as it struck the seventh hour of the morning echoed throughout the silence of the cottage. Cat sat at the kitchen table, her mind running through everything that had been said with Bran and her grandfather.

She'd cooked dinner and managed to get a few bites down before she cleaned up her mess. That led her to doing laundry while scrubbing the bathroom and then moving on to cleaning the entire house. All the while, she attempted to find a way where she could get her grandfather back and help Fintan.

Several times, she found herself turning toward him, only to realize he wasn't there. In a very short time, she'd come to trust and depend on him. She hadn't meant to, but he made it so easy.

Now that he was gone—and it seemed for good—she missed him. He'd blown into her life unexpectedly, and touched her deeply. She'd seen his hurt and the indifference he showed the world.

But then he opened himself up to her. Within his heart, she'd felt his suffering and sensed his capability. He'd overcome so much, and instead of those horrible events making him an alcoholic or druggie, he'd buried everything.

It wasn't exactly the healthiest thing to do, but it was the best of his options. He'd done what he needed to protect himself and move on with his life.

Not that anyone who had been betrayed twice—first by his family, and then Taraeth—ever forgot. Now she was added to the list of betrayers. And it made her feel like the worst kind of person.

As soon as the clock finished chiming, she rose and put on her coat before leaving the house. She couldn't help but look around for Fintan as she walked to the sidewalk, hoping for some indication that he was still around.

She thought she spotted him the alley across from her house and hurried there.

"Fintan," she whispered.

She waited for several minutes, but he didn't show himself—if he was even there. She'd made the right choice. Hadn't she? All she had to do was get her grandfather free of Bran. Then she'd kill the bastard.

For Fintan and herself.

Regret was a painful, bitter pill to swallow. With one last look for Fintan, she turned and headed toward the Garda station. Her path took her past her now burnt café. She paused and looked at the charred remains of the business that had been in her family for three generations.

As she stood there, she became aware of the stares of others around her. It wasn't as if she went out of her way to alienate people, but when her family had been murdered, and she waited to be next, the last thing she thought of was putting a smile on her face and waving to everyone she passed on the street.

She was used to them staring at her oddly or whispering. There were so many rumors about her family circulating that she no longer paid attention to them.

But this was different. There was malice in their eyes and their hearts. Somehow, she'd gone from a quirky local with a peculiar family to someone hated and despised. And she didn't know how.

It was impossible for her not to notice them now. When she happened to look someone in the eye, they hastily looked away. As if she would harm them somehow.

Her attention shifted from the townsfolk when she saw Carmody walking inside the café. She hurried to him, stepping over ash and fallen boards.

"Miss Hayes," he said when he looked up to find her.

She gave him a nod. "I was on my way to see you."

"Oh? And why is that?"

"I want to know if the autopsy from my grandfather is back. I need to know if he was alive when he was burned." It wasn't a complete lie, but she couldn't exactly tell him that she needed to make sure the body actually belonged to her grandfather.

Carmody put his hands on his hips and kicked at a blackened board. "Are you sure you don't know anyone who would want to hurt you?"

"Yesterday, I would've said no one. Then I walked here this morning. By the looks everyone is giving me, I'm glad people aren't hung for suspected witchcraft anymore."

There was a ghost of a smile on his face. "We Irish are a superstitious lot. There are many rumors circulating about your family."

"Always has been. Try growing up here. It could be a harsh

environment for a girl who just wanted to be treated like everyone else."

"I can't imagine," he said. He scratched his chin. "The thing is, I need to know if any of the rumors are true."

It was the first time someone had outright asked her, and somehow, she wasn't surprised that it was Carmody. She looked into his dark eyes and raised a brow. "There are so many. Do you have a specific one you'd like me to verify?"

"Are you a witch?"

She gave a shake of her head and put her hands in her coat pockets. "If I were, would I allow all these bad things to happen to me? My parents' deaths in the accident, my siblings being murdered, my café burning, and now my grandfather."

"The theory sounded better in my head," Carmody said and lowered his gaze, embarrassed. He blew out a breath. "What about the one that says you have Fae blood."

She could tell him the truth, but he wouldn't understand, and would likely take it the wrong way. So she opted for another approach when she saw two Light Fae walking down the street. "Do you believe in the Fae?"

Carmody lifted his gaze and stared at her a long moment before he ran his hands through his blond hair. "Maybe."

"It's a yes or no question, Detective Sergeant. There are those who believe the Fae live among us, right here in Galway."

"Is that what you think?"

She pointed to the two Light who were walking away. "They are here. It's simply a matter of whether you want to believe or not."

"How do you know who is Fae and who isn't?"

"They're almost too beautiful to believe."

He sniffed and rubbed his hand on the back of his neck. "I have a stack of unexplained disappearances and deaths."

"The Fae."

"How?" he asked.

She'd already said too much, but he looked genuinely interested. Still, she wasn't certain. "I don't know."

"You do," he said. "Tell me, and I'll make sure the ruling on the café is completed by the end of the day."

Cat hated that she hadn't seen that coming. "Do I have your word?"

"Yes," he said and held out his hand.

They shook hands. Then she said, "There are two kinds of Fae. Light and Dark. They have their own realm, but a civil war brought them to ours. They chose Ireland as their home."

"How do you know this?" Carmody asked.

She continued without answering. "The Light are relatively easy to spot. They love shiny, pretty things. Generally, they will shop, and occasionally, they'll give in and mate with a human."

"Why do you make that sound like it's a bad thing?"

Cat walked around a heap of melted metal that was once a chair. "Because the Fae are sexual creatures. Humans are drawn to them, enamored by them. The Light are only allowed one night with each human because once we've had a taste of a Fae, no one else will ever be able to give us pleasure again."

The sad part was that, as a Halfling, none of that pertained to her. Yet, she knew deep down that she would never find any sort of ecstasy with anyone but Fintan.

Carmody blinked several times. "And the Dark."

"The Dark you should stay away from at all costs. They walk among us, as well. Many use glamour to hide their red eyes and black and silver hair."

"You're serious," he said, his face going white. "I've seen ones with red eyes before. I thought it was some kind of new contact craze that had become popular."

"I'm afraid not. A Dark's tastes run much nastier than a Light's. The Dark care nothing for frivolities. They live for one thing only. Us."

"I don't understand," Carmody said with a shake of his head.

"The sexual vibe I told you about? The Dark use it against us. They will lure someone to them and give them unimaginable pleasure. The human will crave more and actually beg the Fae. All the while, each time the Dark takes them, they drain a bit of their soul. You see, Detective Sergeant, we're food to them."

He bent over at the waist and propped his hands on his knees. "I think I'm going to be sick."

"Yeah."

"Everyone should know of this," he said as he straightened. "The public needs to be made aware."

She raised a brow at him. "Do you honestly believe the political figures don't have connections to the Fae? You try and put out such a statement, and you'll see how quickly it's shut down."

"I don't understand."

"The Fae live among us. It's a fact. Nothing will change that. They take those who willingly go with them."

"But those humans don't know they're going to their deaths."

She shrugged. "No, they don't. And if you tried to tell them, they wouldn't listen. No one will. The majority of people don't want to admit they already know of the Fae. They want to keep their heads down and go about their lives."

"How do you know so much about the Fae?"

"From my family."

His eyes sharpened as he looked at her. "Have you been targeted because of what you know regarding the Fae?"

"No."

"Do you believe it was a human who torched the café and killed your grandfather?"

Cat hesitated, unsure of how much to tell him. Then again, she'd pretty much told him everything. "No."

"Do you know why a Fae would do these things to you?"

"No." And that was the truth. She had no idea what Bran wanted.

Carmody sighed loudly. "I put a rush on your grandfather's autopsy. The report should be in this morning. Come with me, and I'll get it."

She followed him out of the café. They walked side by side to the Garda station, where he led her to his desk. It was impossible for her not to notice how everyone stared at her.

"Yeah, um, you've become a fascination," Carmody said as he looked around before he sat in his chair.

Cat took the seat in front of his desk. "I'm used to it."

"It's not directed at me, and it bothers me. I don't know how you do it, Miss Hayes."

"We all do things in life we don't like."

He nodded and cleared his throat. Then he stood and set aside some files. "Let me see if the report has come in."

She kept her eyes forward, reading motivational posters and the numerous missing person fliers posted on a corkboard. She tuned out the talk around the station and attempted to remain as patient as her outward appearance when she was anything but.

The clock on the wall ticked by nearly twenty minutes before Carmody returned with a folder in his hand. He had a dazed expression on his face.

He slowly sank into his chair and set the folder in the middle of his desk. Then his gaze lifted to hers.

"What is it?" she asked at his glazed look. "What did you find?"

He rubbed his thumb in a circle against his temple as deep lines formed in his forehead. "The body we found yesterday isn't your grandfather."

Cat closed her eyes and silently screamed her joy. Bran hadn't lied. He'd told her the truth. Which meant she had a decision to make.

The joy she felt turned to acrid smoke, choking her. She was no less prepared for that now than she had been yesterday. In fact, the more she thought about things, the more convoluted they became.

"Miss Hayes?"

She focused on Carmody's face. He was staring at her with concern. She'd been so lost in her thoughts that she wasn't sure if she'd missed a question. "Yes?"

"This is good news."

"In part. Now I need to find my grandfather."

"Who has gone missing?" Carmody's face tightened. "Shall I open an investigation?"

She shook her head and stood. "Thank you for giving me the truth."

"You already suspected the body wasn't your grandfather," he stated as he got to his feet and leaned his hands on either side of the file. "Why didn't you just tell me that?"

"You wouldn't have believed me."

A muscle jumped in his jaw. "And you don't want my help because it involves the F—"

"Thank you," she said over him, silencing his words. "You've been a tremendous help. I'm sure you need to notify the family of whoever was found at my grandfather's."

She turned and walked away before he could ask any more questions.

nineteen

There were many uses for a Fae's ability to veil themselves. Fintan following Cat was one. He trailed her from her home to the café and then inside the Garda station. Now they were headed back to the house.

There had been a couple of instances when she'd left her house that he wanted to drop the veil and let her see him. Especially when she had been looking for him.

But he had a plan. That plan included help from Balladyn, which he knew the other Reapers probably wouldn't like. Fintan was no longer going to stand back and wait to see what Bran would do.

It was time to take action. Bran had caused enough trouble. While Cael hadn't said anything, there was something bothering him. It wasn't like Cael to not be focused. The obvious conclusion was that it had something to do with Bran and Death.

Since Cael was occupied with that, and the others were looking for Eoghan, Fintan was taking the initiative.

He'd told Balladyn everything about Bran, and hopefully, Balladyn would return with some news. Fintan wasn't holding out much hope, though. Bran liked to be in charge. He wouldn't go to the Dark court only to bow to Taraeth.

Whatever Bran had planned for Cat, Fintan was going to be there. He'd intentionally allowed her to think he'd left, mainly because he couldn't be near her and not have her in his arms. She didn't trust him, and he couldn't be with someone who didn't grant him at least that.

Yet every time he thought of losing her either in death or to Bran, it felt as if something were crushing his chest. It was impossible to breathe or even think clearly.

Somehow, someway, Cat had become important to him. And not just to win this war with Bran. No, it was Cat herself. Fintan had known giving in to the yearning of his body and soul would be his undoing. And it had happened in Cat's arms.

Not that he regretted it. She was amazing. In every way. Yes, she'd betrayed him, but in her shoes, would he have done anything differently? She'd been put in a difficult situation involving the last remaining member of her family.

Fintan blew out a breath.

"Fuck," he murmured.

He was furious at her treachery, but if he wanted to make sure she lived, he was going to have to set that aside. He wasn't sure if he could. After previous betrayals, he'd hardened himself to any form of forgiveness.

But this was Cat. She hadn't hurt him because she enjoyed it or because it had gained her power. She'd done it in an attempt to free her grandfather.

There was a good reason for Fintan to remain apart from Cat. If she thought he no longer had her back, then it would come across when Bran questioned her. Because Bran would question her.

It was a good plan, but Fintan knew he couldn't follow through with it. All those centuries of closing off his feelings didn't seem to work around Cat. She'd opened up his heart and soul, and the consequences were only just now coming to light.

His thoughts had changed, and so, too, were his actions. But the one thing that hadn't been altered was his ability to protect her. That he'd do until his last breath.

The return to Cat's house was uneventful. Except for the mortals who stopped and ogled her after she'd walked past. Cat tried to pretend she didn't see them, but Fintan could tell by her hunched shoulders that she was all too aware of what was happening.

He returned to the alley as she entered the house. Shortly after, she yanked the curtains closed. He knew she had to be thinking about Bran and her grandfather. Now that she had confirmation that the body was someone else, it meant she was weighing Bran's request more heavily.

Fintan had no doubt she would go to Bran simply because of her grandfather. If he knew that Bran had Eoghan, Fintan would do the same.

With a sigh, he veiled himself and teleported inside Cat's house. A quick sweep of the dwelling let him know that they were alone. Only then did he drop the veil.

Cat had her back to him as she stood in the kitchen. She set down the glass and slowly turned to him. Her eyes lit up as soon as she saw him.

He wasn't sure what to say. It wasn't until he stood before her once more that he realized why he couldn't shut her out of his life —he'd come to care for her. Greatly.

For a Fae such as him, affection was an emotion none could afford. And yet, he'd somehow developed just that for the Halfling. It wouldn't have mattered if Cat were human. She had the ability to touch him as no one ever had—or ever would.

"I thought you were gone forever," she said.

Fintan glanced at the floor. He rubbed his chest, that invisible band tightening again. Recognizing his growing warmth had only made things worse because he realized how easily he could lose her.

Cat walked toward him, stopping a few feet away. "I'm sorry. I should've told you everything."

"Aye. You should've."

"Tell me I haven't lost you. Please, Fintan. I need you. Not because of Bran, but because...I care about you."

Images of losing her in various, horrific ways kept flashing in his head.

She licked her lips and took a tentative step forward. "I knew if I told you I planned to talk to Bran alone that you'd convince me not to do it. But I had to know his reasons. So I used my magic to create a dome that would hide Bran and me from you. It was seeing you outside of the dome that made him think he could turn me."

"I know," Fintan murmured.

"He believes I betrayed you."

Fintan frowned as he stared into her green eyes. "You did."

"I called to you after. I wanted to tell you everything. I wanted to apologize."

"Because you need my help."

She shook her head of red hair. "I called to you because with you beside me, I don't feel so alone. With you, I feel as if I can conquer whatever is to come."

Damn her for saying all the right things. He held out his hand. She immediately took it, and he pulled her against him. His eyes closed as soon as she wrapped her arms around him. For several minutes, they stayed locked in each other's arms.

"Bran has my grandfather."

Fintan rubbed a hand up and down her back. "I figured that part out."

"It's why I didn't tell you about my talk with Bran inside the dome. I wanted a private place where Bran couldn't hurt me but you couldn't see us."

"The dome."

She nodded her head and leaned back to look at him. "I had the dagger. He couldn't defend himself, and I was about to kill him."

"Then he mentioned your grandfather."

Tears gathered in her eyes. "Yes. I had to know if he spoke the truth."

"I understand." He wiped at the tears that ran down her cheeks. "I shouldn't have veiled myself from you."

"So you were there?"

"I've not left your side."

She sniffed and pressed her cheek against his chest. "Now what? Bran is coming back for me."

"I've got an idea." He pulled her away so he could look into her eyes. "If you had him defenseless once, you can do it again. But that means allowing him to take you wherever he plans."

"And you can follow?" she asked with a frown.

"I will. Nothing will keep me from you."

She wiped her face and straightened her shoulders. "What's the plan?"

"It's better if you don't know details. I'll be with you, though. Always."

He leaned down and pressed his mouth to hers. Their lips parted, and their tongues dueled. He pressed her close to him, needing to feel her warmth and her softness. She was a drug, and he was blissfully addicted.

She ended the kiss and held his face between her hands as she gazed up at him. "I'll never betray you again. Nor will I ever keep anything like this from you. I can't apologize enough for my actions."

"Shh," he said and put a finger over her lips. "We'll get through this. I need to go, but I'll not be far."

"That gives me the courage to face Bran again."

Fintan wanted to kiss her again, but he held himself in check. Instead, he ran his thumb over her bottom lip and veiled himself before returning to the alley across the street.

His musings halted when there was movement beside him as Balladyn appeared. The Dark looked around expectantly. Fintan dropped his veil, causing Balladyn to grin.

"I knew you'd be here," Balladyn said.

Fintan raised a brow. "Why?"

"Because of her," Balladyn said, jutting his chin toward the house.

There was no need to reply, so Fintan didn't bother. "What did you learn?"

"No one knows anything about Bran, but another ten Dark have been reported missing. That's not counting the loners who Bran could've recruited."

Fintan mulled that over. "So his army grows."

"Does Death have an army?"

"She has the Reapers."

One side of Balladyn's mouth lifted. "I see."

"Do you?"

"Very clearly, in fact."

Fintan eyed the Dark. "What is it you think you see?"

"How do you plan to kill Bran?"

He let Balladyn change the subject. "Any way I can. It won't be long before he comes for her."

"Ah. But I still don't believe your interest in the lovely Catriona is solely about Bran." When Fintan didn't respond, Balladyn smiled. "Just as I thought. Not that I blame you. She's a looker with fire in her veins."

Fintan didn't want to discuss Cat in any way. He stared into the Dark's red eyes. "Enough."

Balladyn gave a nod of his head, the grin wiped off his face. "What does Bran want with her?"

"I wish I knew. It has to do with her magic."

The Dark quirked a brow as he shot Fintan a confused look. "Why? What does she have that Bran doesn't?"

"I don't know."

"You mean you didn't take the time to find out?"

Fintan clenched his jaw for a moment. "Up until a few days ago, she believed she didn't have any magic. That was because her grandfather had bound it. When Bran took him, it set her magic free."

"What a fekking mess. Makes me wish I'd been here a few days ago," Balladyn said with a smile. "So she doesn't know how to control her magic?"

Fintan shook his head and looked at Cat's house. There was a shiver of magic that had Fintan turning his head to look behind Balladyn. That's when Kyran appeared while veiled. Fintan's fellow Reaper stayed behind Balladyn, listening.

Balladyn ran a hand over his jaw. "Bran is amassing an army, killing Halflings, and out for revenge against the Reapers and Death. Tell me again why you're involved."

"I never said."

"Right," the Dark stated wryly. "Care to share now?"

"Not particularly."

Balladyn leaned against the brick of the building. There was a long stretch of silence, then he said, "Would you consider returning to court?"

Fintan slowly turned his head to the Dark. "Why?"

"I think you'd be an asset."

"To Taraeth?"

"To me."

It was just as Fintan thought. Balladyn was going to overthrow Taraeth. Part of him wanted to be there to see it, or even be involved after what Taraeth had done to him. But he was a Reaper —and Reapers had other duties.

Fintan blew out a breath. "My time there is done."

"Nothing will bring you back?"

"Nay."

Balladyn's lips twisted. "A pity. If I find out anything about Bran, I'll let you know. Good luck."

No sooner had Balladyn teleported away than Kyran dropped his veil. He raised a brow at Fintan. "Really? Balladyn?"

"We need answers. I was hoping he would be able to help. He did tell me at least ten more Dark have gone missing."

Kyran's lips flattened at the news as his red eyes looked Fintan over. "Does Balladyn know who you are?"

"Of course, not."

"I suspect otherwise. He willingly helped you?"

Fintan shrugged. "He did, though he didn't have much to share."

"Cael filled me in on Cat. Have you made contact with her?"

"Yes." Fintan hoped that was all Kyran would ask.

Kyran looked at him with raised brows. "And?"

"My plan to trap Bran didn't work. In fact, he doesn't want to kill Cat. He wants her help."

Kyran's face scrunched in confusion. "Why? Bran's magic is growing. What use could he have for a Halfling with no magic?"

"She's had magic all along. Her grandfather bound it."

Kyran held up a hand. "Stop. Perhaps you'd better start from the beginning."

Fintan quickly caught Kyran up but made sure to leave out his and Cat's night of passion. The last thing he wanted was to talk about it, when he could barely wrap his head around what had happened.

"Damn," Kyran said, drawing out the word. "If you hadn't stumbled upon Cat, we wouldn't know any of this. And Talin thought you'd have a hard time getting her to open up to you."

Fintan merely shrugged. "She was scared, and I promised to protect her."

"It was the right thing to do."

"Aye." He grew uncomfortable with the way Kyran was staring at him. "Stop it."

"I can't. There's something different about you."

"You're mistaken."

Kyran snorted. "I'm not. This vexes me."

Fintan looked to the sky as he sought patience. "Don't pick up Talin's habits."

"The word fits this scenario."

"Leave it," Fintan stated, glaring at him.

Kyran's frown deepened, and then his eyes widened as his mouth dropped opened.

"Don't," Fintan warned. "Don't say a fekking word."

Kyran's gaze jerked to the house and nodded, letting whatever he was going to say drop. "She lied to you."

"I was there. I know."

"I don't like that," Kyran said as his gaze returned to Fintan.

He shrugged. "She lied for her grandfather. I'd do the same if it were about Eoghan or if it involved any of you."

"Family," Kyran said. "I know all about the things we do for family. Do you care for her?"

Fintan squeezed his eyes closed as he pinched the bridge of his nose with his thumb and forefinger. "I don't want to talk about what I'm feeling or not feeling." He dropped his arm and looked into Kyran's red eyes. "What I want to do is kill Bran."

"You're going to follow her when she goes to Bran."

"Hopefully, I'll be able to stop whatever he has planned and kill him."

Kyran crossed his arms over his chest. "You're going to need help."

"Not this time."

"Especially this time. We've been looking for a way to get to Bran. Do you honestly think any of us is going to let you go after him alone after what happened with Eoghan? We stand together on this."

Fintan shook his head. "One of us has been lost already. We can't gather together in one place for Bran to target all of us again. I have to go alone. If something happens to me, it's just me. Death needs us, whether she or Cael will admit it or not."

"Look, I'm not going ..." Kyran began before his words trailed off while he looked at Cat's house.

Fintan shifted his gaze and found what had caught Kyran's attention. Bran.

"I'm going to kill him," Kyran ground out.

Fintan put a hand on his chest to stop him and veiled both of them. "No. I have a plan."

"It's not a good one."

"You haven't heard all of it," Fintan argued, then hoped Kyran didn't ask to hear it because he had nothing to tell him. "Get to the others. Let them know what happened."

Kyran shook his head. "Fintan, don't."

"This is happening now. There's no time to argue. Do you follow me and leave the others in the dark about what's going on? Or do you tell them?"

"I'm going to kick your arse when this is over," Kyran ground out.

Fintan found himself wanting to grin. "You can try."

"Leave a way we can track you."

"I will." Another lie. Fintan gave Kyran a nod as his friend teleported away.

Then he turned to the house to find Cat at the door, talking to Bran. He wanted to get closer, but he didn't dare. Most likely, Bran had others watching the area.

The only thing that prevented him or Kyran from being discovered was that he'd set up a spell that prohibited anyone from seeing into the alley for just this reason.

He should've known that Bran would come for Cat sooner rather than later. Fintan balled his hands into fists when Bran motioned for Cat to follow him.

She stepped out of the house without her coat. This time, she didn't look for him. Fintan walked from the alley toward them. His blood had begun to boil, the need to wipe out his enemy so great that he could think of nothing else.

It was the sight of Cat's red hair that she flicked over her shoulder that broke through his murderous haze. Fintan halted his steps and squatted a few feet from them. If Bran sent any magic out, it would miss Fintan.

"Are you ready?" Bran asked her.

Cat lifted her chin. "Yes."

Fintan whispered her name, linking him to her.

Bran held out his hand. As soon as she took it, they disappeared. Now that Fintan could track Cat, he was right behind them.

He half expected wards to be up, preventing him from following, yet there was nothing. That wasn't like Bran at all. When Fintan arrived at the veiled, lavish manor and looked around, he immediately knew something was wrong.

It wasn't until he tried to teleport that he realized what it was.

Bran had set a trap for him.

CHAPTER
twenty

The maniacal laughter sent chills of dread racing over Cat's skin. She turned in a circle, looking for Bran, but he was nowhere to be found.

Then her gaze landed on metal bars. It was the person behind them that made her stomach drop to her feet.

"Fintan," she whispered.

She could only stare at him in dismay and alarm. Fintan didn't flinch, didn't contort his face in anger. In fact, he stood there as if there weren't bars surrounding him.

All the time she believed Fintan had abandoned her, and he'd been right there. She should've known. He'd given his word. It was just that she was so used to others who didn't think twice about going back on their promise that she'd assumed the same about him.

He wasn't like others. Not by a long shot. He'd shown her that so many times in so many ways. If only she'd had faith in him from the beginning. If only she hadn't lied to him.

If only ...

She looked into his red-rimmed white eyes and was glad they'd had the time so she could apologize. Though it wasn't enough. It would never be enough. Just as she wished she could've told him how she craved his nearness, his touch. His voice.

"Well, well, well," Bran said as he appeared beside her.

Cat jerked away, more wary of him than ever. Bran cut his silver eyes to her, but his attention was on Fintan—who she had unknowingly led right into a trap.

"Of all the Reapers I thought I might catch, I believed you were smarter than this," Bran said to Fintan as he neared the cage. "A pity, really. I had high hopes for you."

Fintan's expression remained impassive. He stayed calm and unfazed. "Let me ease whatever questions you might pose regarding my loyalty. I'm a Reaper. I pledged myself to Death. I follow Cael in all things. I stand by my brothers and sisters. Not you. Never you."

She wanted to cheer as Fintan eloquently stated the words. Had she been in his place, she would've allowed her anger to get the better of her and would have shouted her thoughts, laced heavily with vulgarities. Nothing made her feel like she got the point across without a few choice cuss words thrown in.

But not Fintan. He'd shown her another way. She only knew he was livid because she'd heard the hate in his voice when he'd spoken of Bran before. A stranger would assume that he was utterly indifferent, but she knew the truth.

Bran's head turned to her. Cat liked it better when his focus was elsewhere. Right now, he had not one, but two people she would do anything for.

And she feared that Bran knew it.

"What does he mean to you?" Bran asked and jerked his head toward Fintan.

Cat kept her gaze on Bran to reinforce her words. "As I told you before, Fintan offered to keep me alive, as well as promised to prevent you from taking me."

"Ah." Bran faced her and smiled. "Did he vow to kill me?"

"He wants to, but he made no such promises.

Bran's smile widened. "The ever pragmatic Fintan."

"How do you know so much about him?" she demanded.

"I make it my business to know everything about my enemies."

Somehow, she didn't think that statement was entirely truthful. Bran might very well have learned a lot about Fintan, but she doubted that he knew everything.

"Does that statement also include Death?"

Bran grinned. "Curious about her, are you?"

Cat nodded. "Humans portray Death as a tall, cloaked, skeletal figure with a scythe. And it's assumed that Death is male."

"Death is something else entirely, but you'll get to see that for yourself shortly."

Apprehension tightened her stomach. "What do you mean?"

"Haven't you guessed, my dear? You're here to bring Death to me."

Cat took a step back before she realized it. She shook her head at Bran, panic and trepidation clawing at her. "I won't help you kill Death."

"Sure you will," Bran said without missing a beat.

She gawked at him. He was so sure of himself that it gave her pause. She glanced at Fintan to see his gaze fastened on his enemy.

Despite knowing what Bran's response would be, she lifted her chin and said, "No."

"So many innocents have died," Bran said. "I went after

Halflings simply because I wanted to. And because I knew it would infuriate Death." He leaned toward her and said in a loud whisper, "I hate her, you see."

Cat stared into the eyes of a lunatic. A certifiable madman with delusions of gradeur.

"She took a life, and she must pay for it," Bran stated.

Cat shook her head. "She's Death. And she has rules, rules that you agreed to."

Instead of becoming angry, Bran laughed. "I see Fintan has totally gotten you to drink the Reaper Kool-Aid. A pity, really. Now, I'm going to have to use force to get you to see my side."

"I see your side."

"Hardly. When I accepted Death's offer, I'd been ruthlessly betrayed and killed. I wasn't ready to die. I wanted to live. And she gave me that chance with added magic and power that I could feel running just beneath my skin. I would've agreed to anything."

Cat rubbed her thumb along her fingers at her side at the mention of the feel of magic. She longed to sense it within herself. "I suspect anyone would be overjoyed at the prospect of coming back to life."

"But she put so many restrictions in place," Bran said irritably. "Thousands of years of loneliness, of needing something I could neither name nor understand. Until I met Anorrya. I loved her the moment I looked at her, and I knew I couldn't live without her."

Cat fought not to slide her gaze to Fintan to see his reaction. She nodded in understanding. "I know loneliness."

"I kept my relationship with Anorrya secret for nearly a year, but then I grew tired of that. I wanted her with me, to be a part of my life. So I told her everything."

"Didn't you know Death would kill her?" Cat asked.

Bran's silver eyes narrowed. "I thought Death would speak to me first."

"It wouldn't matter what she did. You'd hate her either way."

"Are you saying I shouldn't loathe her?"

Cat shrugged and nodded. "The blame lies solely on your shoulders."

"Does it?"

Once more, Bran's calm reply confused her. Most people would be angry and shouting at this point. It was almost as if he were leading her to one conclusion. And she was hesitantly playing along. "You knew the rules."

"Rules. Yes, rules are important." He looked at the floor and walked slowly around her.

She watched Bran, never taking her eyes off him. He was up to something, and she wanted to be prepared for it. To see how far she could push her magic, she silently wished that her dagger were in her hand but hidden from Bran's view.

A heartbeat later, she felt the weight of the hilt in her grip. Cat hurriedly turned the weapon so the blade rested along the inside of her arm.

Bran quirked a brow. "Those rules you spoke of are no longer in place. Didn't you hear Fintan? He said he was loyal to his brothers and sisters."

"I heard."

"Death made concessions for this new set of Reapers. Why couldn't she do the same for me?"

"I don't know," Cat said.

Bran stopped before her, their toes inches apart. He leaned his face close to hers and said conspiratorially. "Let's ask her."

"I don't think that's wise."

"I do. And I always get what I want."

It was on the tip of her tongue to mention that he no longer had Anorrya, but Cat wisely kept her mouth shut. There was no need to poke the beast.

Not yet anyway.

"Call for Death," Bran ordered.

Cat shook her head. "I won't."

Bran smiled and snapped his fingers. Almost instantly, Searlas and her grandfather appeared on the far side of the room.

She knew with a sinking heart what Bran planned to do, and she loathed him for it.

"Call for Death, or I kill your grandfather."

Cat lifted her chin, defiance in every fiber of her being. "Our deal was that I help you, and you let my grandfather return—alive —to his cottage."

"Perhaps," Bran said with a sinister grin, "I've changed my mind. I think I'll keep your grandfather right here to ensure that you do just what I want."

Her grandfather quickly said, "Don't do it, a stóirín."

Searlas backhanded him so hard that he fell to the ground. Cat tried to go to her grandfather, but Bran grabbed hold of her arm, keeping her in place. She jerked her bicep out of his grasp and stepped away from him.

"I despise you," she stated angrily.

Bran shrugged. "I suspected as much. You can try to send your grandfather to safety or even attempt to remove someone else in this room, but you'll find that I've prevented it. Others can come to us. But no one leaves."

Her mind raced with possibilities. There was no way she would bring Death to Bran so he could kill her. There had to be another way.

"What's it going to be, Catriona?" Bran asked as he strolled to her grandfather and walked a circle around him and Searlas. "Will you bring me Death, or will you watch me kill your sole family member slowly and painfully?"

Searlas jerked her grandfather to his feet. Her grandfather wiped at the trickle of blood from the corner of his mouth. His green eyes met hers as he silently repeated his words from earlier.

He was asking the impossible.

"Last chance," Bran said. "Will you bring me Death?"

Cat swallowed, tears filling her eyes. "No."

Her grandfather's smile was wide as pride shone in his gaze.

"So be it," Bran said.

Cat's knees buckled when her grandfather doubled over and cried out in pain. She tried to go to him, but once more, Bran prevented it. When her grandfather fell to the floor, wracked in agony, Cat's knees buckled.

She hit the floor hard, but she didn't feel it. She felt nothing. For the next ten minutes, she listened to her grandfather's screams before the last bit of life drained from him.

She remained kneeling on the floor. There were no more tears to cry, no more words to scream. She had done the unthinkable and caused the last remaining member of her family to be murdered.

Hate burned inside her. She detested herself, but most of the abhorrence was directed at Bran.

"I really thought you'd do what I wanted," Bran said with a look of disbelief and acceptance. "But that's all right since we have someone else you care about."

While Cat had watched her grandfather die, she'd already figured out Bran's next move. It was no surprise that he now threatened Fintan.

"I was willing to do anything for my grandfather," Cat said

without looking at Bran, who walked to Fintan's cage. "What makes you think I'd do the same for him?"

There was a brief pause. "You mean you don't care about Fintan?"

She wanted to reach inside Bran's chest and rip out his heart, to crush it into nothingness. She wanted to see him suffer the most horrible and cruelest of punishments for five hundred years before he was allowed to die. She wanted him to beg and plead for his life in a place where no one would ever hear him.

"You think I care about him because I trusted him?" she asked. Cat then got to her feet and faced Bran. She didn't look at Fintan, because if she did, she wasn't sure she'd be able to carry out her plan. "You're wrong. I barely know Fintan."

Bran's brows lifted high in his forehead as he studied her. "I do believe you're telling the truth."

"I'm not going to bring Death to you."

Bran smiled and nodded. "You will, Cat."

"Who are you going to threaten this time? The entire population of Galway? The world? Do it. See if I care."

In a blink, Bran was before her, his hand around her throat, squeezing tightly as his face loomed over hers. The fury she'd been expecting to see earlier blazed in his silver eyes. "You're going to do what I want."

She smiled at him. All the while, she let a single wish drift through her mind.

CHAPTER

twenty-one

As soon as Kyran appeared within the concrete walls of the fortress, he began shouting for everyone. Within seconds, the others stood before him. He searched faces until his gaze landed on Cael.

"What happened?" Cael demanded.

"The absolute worst." Kyran raked his hand through his black and silver hair and paced the length of the spacious room. "I knew we were all affected by what happened with Eoghan, but the one I didn't worry about was Fintan."

Cael took a step away from the others. "What happened?" he asked again, this time in a low tone, signaling that his patience was running out.

Kyran halted. "I tried to talk him out of it."

"We're sure you did," Talin said. "Just tell us what happened."

Kyran met Cael's silver gaze. "Fintan's plan to trap Bran back-fired. Bran knew all along who Cat was, and he never intended to kill her."

"Why the hell not?" Baylon demanded.

This was the part Kyran dreaded telling. "Bran wants Cat for something."

"And he was using her to trap a Reaper," Cael concluded.

Kyran nodded, anger twisting his gut. "Cat has magic. She had it all along."

"I know," Cael said. "Her magic is nearly as strong as a full-blood Fae's. Because of it, her grandfather bound it when she was just a baby. When Bran then took the grandfather, it broke that binding."

"So she has her magic once more. What all can she do?" Neve asked.

Kyran pinched the bridge of his nose with his thumb and fore-finger. "She has only to wish for something, and it happens."

"A Fae can do that," River said. "What's so special about this half-Fae?"

Kyran wished he had an answer. He could only stare at his woman and shrug. "Since Bran was holding Cat's grandfather, she went with him. And Fintan followed."

"Why the hell didn't you say that to begin with?" Talin shouted.

Cael's gaze lowered to the floor. "Because Fintan doesn't want us there."

"I don't fekking care what he wants," Baylon said. "We need to be there."

Cael turned and faced the group. "After what happened with Eoghan, Fintan is trying to protect the rest of us. He knows that you three have your women."

Talin expelled a loud sigh. "I'm vexed. I don't like this. Any of this."

"We aren't really going to let Fintan handle this on his own, are we?" Jordyn asked as she looked from Baylon to the others.

Kyran frowned as he felt something tug at him. It was soft, like a whisper. He gave a shake of his head when it disappeared and once again concentrated on the conversation.

"We can find Fintan," Neve said.

Talin glanced at his woman. "You're not going anywhere near Bran."

"Excuse me?" Neve put her hands on her waist where dozens of knife handles peeked out from their sheaths in her corset. "Did you forget that I'm a Reaper now? Did you forget what Bran did to my parents? My brother?"

"No," Talin said and tried to keep talking, but Neve's voice rose as she spoke over him.

"I deserve retribution against that maniac just as much as any of you."

Kyran felt the tug again. It was stronger, like a hand on his arm. He glanced down but saw nothing. Was he losing his mind?

"What is it?" River whispered as she came to stand beside him.

He looked into her pale blue eyes. "I don't know."

"Something isn't right."

His gaze lowered to where her hand rested over the slight swell of her belly where their child grew. "You're safe here. We put up enough protection spells to ensure that."

She raised a dark brow. "Would it keep Death out?"

He hesitated.

"That's what I thought," River said. "Bran's power is growing. Nothing will keep him out if he finds this place."

"He won't," Cael said.

Kyran jerked his head to Cael. "You sound sure of it."

"I am. In Fintan's place, I would've demanded you not come with me either," Cael said. "Bran wants us all together once more. It's his chance to wipe us out and get to Death."

Jordyn was the one to ask, "You wouldn't be saying that if Erith were all right. She isn't, is she?"

"She's worried about how Bran is getting his power."

Kyran knew Cael was lying. He didn't know about which part, but when it came to Death, Cael went out of his way to protect her. In any other scenario, Kyran would think Cael had an interest in Erith, but that wasn't Cael or Death.

"I'm not leaving Fintan alone to fight Bran," Baylon said.

Kyran covered River's hand with his own as he looked into her eyes and said to the group, "I'm going after Fintan."

"Neither of you is," Cael stated. "I—"

There was a rushing sound that drowned out everything. Kyran reached for River, but she faded from his grasp like smoke. The next time he blinked, he was standing in a room, staring at Cat and Bran.

Kyran looked around and saw the other Reapers—including Daire. Then he saw Fintan, who stood within the confines of a metal cage. Searlas stood on the other side of the room next to a dead mortal.

The fact that Bran and Searlas didn't notice them meant that they were veiled. But who had sent them? His gaze slid to Cat.

Perhaps he should be asking who brought them?

As one, the six of them spread out around the room as they watched Bran tighten his fingers around Cat's throat as he peeled back his lips in a snarl.

Kyran looked at Fintan, who stood still as stone, seething with unleashed fury—all of it directed at Bran.

"Why are you smiling?" Bran asked Cat as he narrowed his eyes at her.

When she didn't answer, he squeezed tighter, causing her face to lose color, but she never let the grin slip from her lips.

A full minute passed before Bran loosened his fingers and shoved her away. "I'll kill Fintan."

"You can annihilate the entire realm, and I still wouldn't bring Death to you," she said with anger dripping from every syllable. Cat's smile was gone, and she looked at Bran as if the very sight of him made her ill. "You're a spoiled child who didn't like the rules and tried to go around them. When you got caught and were subsequently punished, you blamed everyone but the one responsible. You."

Kyran's gaze moved between Cat and Bran. She was pushing him too hard, and if she didn't stop, she was going to feel the consequences of Bran's wrath very soon.

Cat tilted her head to the side and tucked her red hair behind her ear. Already, bruises were beginning to appear on her pale skin from Bran's grip.

Fintan's rage was palpable, filling the room. He had yet to take his gaze off Bran, but Kyran knew that Fintan was all too aware of Cat's every movement, every thought, and every word.

"Why don't you bring Death here?" Cat asked Bran. She widened her eyes and held up her hands with a shrug. "Is it because you can't? The great, powerful Bran? Surely, you can do whatever you want. Didn't you kill Eoghan?"

Bran's lips twisted in a nasty sneer. "If only Eoghan was dead."

"So you couldn't even manage that?" Cat said and shook her head mockingly.

"There was interference by another Fae. A pesky Light that I'll soon take care of."

Cat barked in laughter. "You expect me to believe that when you can't kill a Reaper or bring Death to you? Really, what can you do?"

A glance at the other Reapers told Kyran that all of them were ready for the explosion they knew was coming. Even Searlas had taken several steps back.

Bran threw back his head and roared as he held out his fists at his sides. Then his gaze locked on Cat. She was thrown backward through a window. Glass shattered in every direction. She lay still upon the ground with her red hair spread around her.

There was a moment of silence before she slowly rolled and rose to her hands and knees. The sound of glass hitting glass as it fell from her filled the quiet. Then she got to her feet and faced Bran. She didn't say a word as she walked back into the house to stand before him once more.

She shook out her hair, dislodging dozens of tiny fragments. Ignoring the various cuts all over her, she met Bran's gaze. "A child acts out because he doesn't know how to handle his emotions. A man—be it mortal or Fae—would know how to channel such things into words."

"I've tried to be nice to you. That didn't work. So I've shown you another side of me," Bran said.

Kyran crept closer as Cat gave Bran a look of contempt. "Nice?" she asked. "You've been anything but. You've killed my siblings, torched my café, and kidnapped my grandfather. Then you threatened and bribed me, to try and get me to do what you wanted. Just because it was all done with a smile doesn't mean you were nice. You don't know the meaning of the word."

"And you don't know when to shut up, do you?" Bran asked.

Kyran was thinking the same thing. It was like Cat wanted to push Bran to the breaking point. All it was doing was putting her in harm's way.

Cat wiped at a trickle of blood that fell from her temple. "Why haven't you killed me? You seem like the type of fella who slits people's throats for displeasing you. I think I'm still alive because you need me."

Cael was shaking his head as he moved closer to Fintan's cage with Daire. Kyran realized that Cat had indeed brought them there, and she was trying to get Bran to disclose why she was so important to his plans.

Unfortunately, it might cost Cat her life.

"You could've been a good asset," Bran said.

Cat glanced upward as she shrugged and sighed. "I've been a constant disappointment to everyone. It's the one thing I excel at. Perhaps had you done better research, you'd have known that."

"What I know about you, Cat, is that you're confined to the mortal world." There was a sly grin on Bran's face. "You have powers enough that you should have a place with the Fae."

Step by step, the Reapers were shifting positions. Baylon moved behind Searlas. Talin and Neve came up on either side of Bran. Kyran moved closer to Cat to be able to reach her, while Cael and Daire worked to find the door to release Fintan.

Cat looked at the prone body of the mortal by Searlas's feet. "I had a place I belonged. You took that from me."

"I'm giving you another opportunity."

She raised a brow and looked at Bran curiously. "How so?"

"I'm going to kill Death. It'll happen much sooner with your help, but I'll do it regardless."

"You talk big for a Fae who sought help from a Halfling."

Bran's smile grew. "I talk like any conqueror."

"You've still not told me why you need me."

Kyran silently rooted for Cat. She kept bringing the conversation back to the one thing they all wanted to know.

Bran eyed her silently for a long, tense moment. "I'm surprised you've not figured it out."

"If Fintan was right when he told me you were gaining in power, then I don't know," Cat said. She tapped her finger on her chin as her brow furrowed. "Unless ... you're stealing Death's power somehow. It's why she's not found you herself and killed you. And why you can't find her."

Bran lifted his hands and clapped once, twice. "Very perceptive."

"But why me? Why not another Fae?"

"Because your magic exceeds most Fae. Now, tell me, Catriona—and you need to think carefully about this because Searlas will snuff out your life if you don't speak the truth—did you keep me talking in the hopes that someone might come save you?"

Kyran called for his sword at the same time as the other Reapers. His hand hovered over Cat's arm, ready to yank her away.

"Yes," Cat replied with a serene smile.

"Were you really that stupid?" Bran asked with a laugh.

Her smile grew. "Yes."

As one, the Reapers dropped their veils.

twenty-two

Fintan could no longer wait for Cael and Daire to find the door. He wasn't even sure there was one to his cell. But he had to get to Cat.

He clenched and unclenched his hands. His muscles felt confined by his skin. There was a pounding in his ears, and everything faded from his sight except for one person—Cat.

Kyran yanked her out of the way before Bran could kill her with a bubble of magic. Then, all hell broke loose.

With the adrenaline rushing through his veins, Fintan called to his magic. He felt it gather within him like a whirlpool, one that gained strength and speed by the second.

As his magic built and grew, he narrowed his focus on the bars holding him. The clang of swords and the grunts as weapons and magic made contact drifted around him. He thought of Cat and all she'd sacrificed. He thought of Eoghan and the other Reapers.

And his magic expanded, sharpened.

It cut through the steel cage without any resistance. The cell disintegrated into nothing. Fintan held out his hand and called to his sword.

As soon as he felt the weight of the pommel in his hand, he rushed into the battle. While he'd been absorbed with freeing himself, Bran had called to some of his men.

Fintan cut through Fae after Fae as he searched the room for any sign of Cat. He dodged magic and weapons, taking pleasure each time his sword sank into an opponent.

He didn't linger on the fact that the same Dark would eventually rise again. Bran had twisted the power he'd been taking from Death into something dark and evil before passing it on to his army.

As usual, the Reapers were outnumbered, but they still managed to take down numerous Fae. Because they fought for justice and love and their way of life.

They fought for Death.

Magic crashed into him from behind. The force of it propelled Fintan forward, dropping him to one knee. Tendrils of smoke drifted around his head as he straightened. He slowly turned, his gaze clashing with Bran's.

"I'm going to win!" Bran shouted.

All the while, Cael was coming up behind Bran. Fintan held out his arms and motioned for Bran to come at him. With Bran's attention distracted, Cael just might get enough of an advantage to end Bran once and for all.

Bran took two steps toward him before Cael plunged his sword into Bran's back. Fintan smiled, joy filling him at the thought of their enemy being vanquished and life returning to normal.

But it wasn't Bran's cry of pain that was heard. It was his bark of laughter. And it ceased the battle immediately. Bran looked down at the sword protruding from his chest and laughed louder.

Cael twisted the blade, but nothing seemed to faze Bran. It was like he didn't feel pain.

As if he couldn't be killed.

Cael withdrew the sword and struck again. But once more, nothing happened.

"Enough!" Bran bellowed as he took a step forward, extracting himself from the weapon. He held his hand high and turned in a circle.

Fintan watched as Bran's army faded away, leaving only him and Searlas against seven Reapers. There was movement behind Kyran. Fintan held his breath as he waited to see if it was Cat.

As soon as he spotted her red hair, he wanted to go to her. Fintan held himself in check and returned his attention to Bran, who was shaking his head at them.

"Don't any of you get it?" Bran asked. "I'm in charge now."

Cael gave a loud, derisive snort. "Not as long as Death is alive."

"Oh, that will be taken care of soon," Bran stated.

Fintan saw how Kyran and Talin were shielding Cat from Bran's view. If he couldn't get to Death, and Death couldn't get to him, then each had to have someone kill the other for them.

"Once more jumping the gun, aye?" Cael asked.

Bran looked down and touched the hole in his clothes from Cael's sword. "You can try to kill me all you want. It isn't going to happen. My strength equals Erith's now. Soon, I'll have more. She'll only be able to hide for so long."

"You think she's hiding?" Neve asked.

Bran's head swung to her. His nostrils flared as anger sizzled in his eyes. "It looks like you got all you wanted."

Neve rolled her eyes. "You're an idiot. A complete and utter imbecile."

"Because I gave you the ability to be a Reaper?"

Fintan glanced at Talin to see his hands clenched and his teeth bared. It was only Kyran's hand on his arm that held Talin back.

"You're an idiot if you really think you did me a favor," Neve stated. "You slaughtered my parents in front of me. You turned my brother Dark and had him kill me."

Bran laughed as he walked toward her. "Ah. That was a brilliant plan. Seeing it come together was perfection."

"Neve," Cael said when she made to lunge at Bran.

Bran wagged his finger at her. "I can't die. But you can. Think about that before you attack."

"Liar," Cat declared.

Fintan briefly closed his eyes when he heard Cat's voice. She pushed Talin and Kyran aside and went to Bran, not stopping until she was a foot from him.

Bran raised a brow as he gazed down at her curiously. "For someone just coming into this game, you sure presume to know a lot, little Halfling."

"You brought me into this. You're to blame."

Fintan really wished she'd stop provoking Bran. She moved to walk around Bran, much as he had done with her earlier, and her gaze met Fintan's.

In that brief second in time, Finan saw much in her emerald eyes. Regret for lying to him, grief for her grandfather's death, sadness at sacrificing him, and an eagerness for revenge.

He gave her a slight nod to let her know he trusted her. He always had, and he should've told her that from the beginning. She wasn't the only one who had apologies to make, but that was for later.

Cat had put much together already that none of them had. Apparently, she'd figured something else out. It was easier for her since she saw the big picture while the rest of them were hampered with the past and focused on Bran.

It had given Bran an advantage until now. And Fintan inwardly smiled as he realized Bran was probably regretting approaching Cat.

Bran's smile didn't appear as carefree as before. His head swiveled as he watched Cat walk around him. "What do you think you know?"

"A lot."

Bran folded his arms over his chest as he gave Cat an indifferent look. "I doubt that. Now, stop this foolishness and come with me."

"Or you'll kill Fintan?" she asked curiously.

There was a small hesitation before he replied, "Exactly."

"If you want to wipe out the Reapers, why haven't you already? You had him," she said, pointing to Fintan.

And then it struck Fintan.

Bran couldn't kill them. It's why in their clashes, none of the Reapers had been killed.

"Yes," Fintan said as he stepped forward. "Why didn't you kill me?"

Bran looked from Cat to him. "You can't be that dumb. I was using you as leverage against her."

"You did with her grandfather, as well. That was her blood, her family, and she wouldn't join you. You didn't really think she would cave for me, did you?" Fintan watched the way Bran began to look uncomfortable.

Bran dropped his arms to his sides. "Of course, I did."

"Liar," Cat said again.

Cael's sword vanished as he walked to Bran, forcing him to face Cael until they were nose to nose. "You are a speck of dust beneath Death's shoe. You betrayed your brothers and our cause. You should've died that day. I should've killed you."

"But Erith stopped you," Bran said with a small grin.

Cael's lips peeled back. "Everything Cat said is true. Neither you nor Death can find the other. We can't kill your army, and you can't kill us because we're Death's."

"Shall I clap for you for figuring it all out with the help of a Halfling?" Bran asked. He snorted. "If it weren't for Cat, none of you would know any of this."

Fintan's lips parted when he saw the glint of light off a blade as Cat turned the hilt over so the dagger pointed down.

Without vacillating, she thrust the blade up and between Bran's ribs. Fintan rushed to her, tackling her to the ground and shielding her body with his, as Searlas and Bran both directed magic at her.

Fintan didn't care how excruciating the orbs of magic were as they landed upon him. He was looking into clear, emerald eyes. There were shouts around him, but he heard none of it. He was sinking into a sea of green.

He didn't feel the pain. Not when he was touching Cat again. She had seen him for a man and not a monster. She had touched not just his skin, but also his soul. She had accepted everything he was without judgment or question.

If he'd known how to react, he might have said or done the right thing so she would trust him. Even as he wished things were different between them, he knew it was for the best.

He couldn't contain or control the emotions she brought out in him. Too many centuries had passed with him burying them for him to dig them out now.

When he'd been locked in the cage and listening to her with Bran, Fintan had realized that Cat was meant for so much more than him. She was clever and powerful. Because of her association with him, she no longer had any family.

He'd said his good-byes to her then. With her magic returned and no one to stand in her way, there was much she could accomplish for herself and others. No matter how much he wanted to stay with her, he had to let her go.

And it was going to kill him to do it.

It was the quiet that finally penetrated his thoughts. He looked over his shoulder to find the others watching him. Fintan rolled off Cat and stood before giving her a hand up.

"What happened?" she asked.

Neve rolled her eyes. "The arse got away."

"But you wounded him," Cael said. "How did you know it would work?"

Cat grinned sheepishly. "I'm not part of Death's army. Since he was so adamant that I bring Death here, I began to think he might want me to kill her, as well."

"So you took a chance?" Fintan asked.

She nodded. "I figured there was a very good chance I was right."

"We're lucky you thought of that," Kyran said.

Daire looked to Cael. "I think Bran is going after Rhi soon."

"Go to her," Cael ordered.

With that, Daire teleported out. Now that Bran was gone, his spell no longer held. Which meant they could all return home.

Home. That word meant something different now. He associated it with Cat. It was those damn emotions again. He couldn't even look at her without being sucked under.

"We need to get back," Kyran said. "River and Jordyn are going to be worried."

Fintan saw Cael about to agree, so he hurried and said, "I have some things to attend to. Can someone escort Cat home?"

"I'll do it," Cael said.

It took two tries before Fintan was able to look her way. He bowed his head but didn't attempt any words. They would sound foolish even if he could get them out. It was better if he kept them locked inside with his emotions.

When he turned around, Cael was watching him intently. No doubt he would have questions later. And when Fintan had his emotions buried once more, he would be able to answer them.

Fintan turned his back to Cat and everything they'd share. Being with her and nearly losing her to Bran had shown him that he couldn't allow any feelings to rise—not even the love he had for her.

It was too painful, too ... agonizing. To have any sort of joy with her only to lose her would rip him in two. He silenced his heart with a single thought, though he could do nothing about the anguish that reverberated within him.

Then he teleported away.

twenty-three

So this is what it felt like to have your heart shredded.

Cat blinked, her mind frozen as she stared at where Fintan had been standing. Except ... he was gone. Probably forever.

There was so much she wanted to say. And he hadn't let her.

Not that she blamed him. She deserved it after lying to him.

Still, it made her feel like shite. Worse because she thought they had gotten over her betrayal. She should've realized that what he'd suffered before would leave scars that never fully healed. And she had added another.

The fact that the other Reapers were staring at her didn't alleviate her anguish or distress. She tried not to fidget, but it was a habit when she got uncomfortable.

And she had skyrocketed past uneasy and was now in uncharted territory.

"I'm Cael," said a Fae with long, black hair and silver eyes. "I know Fintan told you about us."

She nodded and glanced at the female who stood tall and beautiful with her inky hair that was divided into five thick braids from her face to her neck before being gathered into one. She wore skintight black from head to foot and tall black boots that went over her knees. There were gauntlets as well as a leather corset that had several knives poking out.

"I'm Neve," the Fae said with a smile. Then she looked at the Light beside her. "And this is my Talin."

Talin wrapped an arm around Neve before he told Cat, "Hello."

Cael then pointed to the remaining Fae, one a Dark and the other a Light. "That is Kyran and Baylon. Daire was the first to leave."

"Thank you for all that you did," Kyran said.

Cat looked down at the dagger in her hand and saw the blood dripping off it. "I think I'd like to go home now." She raised her eyes. "Unless I can't. Fintan told me that Death kills any Fae who knows about you."

"You're a Halfling," Cael said.

She wasn't sure what that meant, and she didn't ask. She just wanted to go home and soak in the tub to help warm her, though she wasn't sure that would ever happen now.

Ever since Fintan left, she'd been cold. As if freezing from the inside out.

If only she had Fintan's arms around her ...

"Ready?"

Cat blinked to focus her eyes. While her thoughts had been on Fintan, Cael had moved beside her. By his look, this wasn't the first time he'd asked if she were ready.

"Yes," she mumbled.

He put his hand on her, and in the next second, she was

standing outside her front door. She moved to go inside when his voice stopped her.

"I know you could've returned on your own. Why didn't you?"

Her shoulders sagged as she faced the leader of the Reapers. "I don't know."

"I think it's because you're not quite ready to see the last of a certain Reaper. We're your link to Fintan."

She hastily looked away from Cael's knowing, silver eyes.

He drew in a deep breath. "Fintan is a unique individual. He's broken in a lot of ways, but he refused to remain that way. He put his pieces back together, albeit roughly. The only way he could get on with his life was by burying his feelings. Despite that, he is one of the most loyal men I've ever known."

"I lied to him." Despair and regret rose so quickly that it choked her. "No apology will ever make up for that."

Cael reached around her and opened the door. "May I?"

She nodded and walked inside with him on her heels. Cat went to the table and set the dagger down before sinking into a chair.

Cael took the seat opposite her. "Fintan has accepted your apology."

"Then why did he leave?" she asked, confusion gripping her.

"Because of his feelings for you. He suppressed every ounce of emotion in order to get past his betrayals. You made him feel again, and it terrifies him."

A tear fell down her cheek. Then a second followed. Someone so wonderful and beautiful had come into her life, and she'd ruined it all with a lie.

"I feel like such a fool." She sniffed, fighting back more tears.

Cael leaned back in the chair with one arm on the table. "The way I see it, you have a couple of choices. One, you can let him go."

"He left," she interrupted .

Cael stared at her a long time, his gaze searching, intense. He must have found what he looked for because he said, "Fintan left because his feelings run deep, and he fears losing you."

She frowned in confusion. Then it dawned on her. "Because I'm mortal."

"Aye."

She snorted and shoved her hair out of her face. "I've drawn blood from a being that has as much power as Death. Bran will be coming for me."

"I'm aware of that, and I'll do what I can to protect you."

She hadn't been expecting such an offer after what she'd done to Fintan. "You would do that?"

"Of course."

She turned her head and looked out the window, hoping for a glimpse of Fintan. "I got so used to seeing Fintan around that it feels wrong not to have him near."

"I suppose the close proximity brought the two of you together?"

Her gaze slid to Cael. She knew what he was asking, and even though who she took to her bed was her business, she said, "It did. He told me of his past, and I told him of mine."

Cael's eyes grew round in surprise. "He spoke of his past?"

"All of it," she said with a nod.

"He's never told anyone. Not even me."

She looked down at her hands and felt the tears coming again. "Did he ever tell you that none of the Fae females would have anything to do with him? They shunned him." She looked up at Cael. "Him? Of all the Fae. They should've been begging for his affection."

"You showed Fintan a sort of kindness and care he's never had."

And it was killing her to know that she might never see him again. She sniffed loudly. "You said I had a couple of options."

"Yes, but it'll depend on how badly you want it," Cael said.

That got her attention. She sat up straighter. "Tell me."

"Go to him."

It would give her a chance to say everything she wanted, but there had to be a catch. "Why would you tell me that?"

"I'm doing it for Fintan," Cael said. "He deserves happiness, but only if you're sincere. Fintan is the type that once he cuts off his emotions, you'll likely not get them back again."

She shoved back the chair and stood. "Then I need to get to him quickly."

Cael was slower to rise. "I don't think I need to tell you what I'll do to you—what all the Reapers will do—if you hurt him. If you're not positive about this—about him—then don't do it."

"If you're asking if I love him, I've already fallen for him. I hate that I didn't trust him. I miss him so much that my chest aches. It's as if I have a hole there. I want to be near him, to look into his eyes."

Cael smiled as he moved aside and pushed in his chair. "Good luck, then."

"Wait," she called when he started to turn away. "Aren't you taking me to him?"

Cael turned back to her with a smile. "You don't need me, Halfling."

"Oh." It was going to take her a while to get used to having magic. Her smile grew as she realized she'd had the power all along to go to Fintan.

Cael had just wanted to make sure she was worthy of his brother. And she hoped she was.

She let thoughts of Fintan fill her mind before she whispered, "I wish I was with Fintan."

In the next moment, she found herself standing on a beach. About fifty yards ahead of her was Fintan, who stood facing the water and the magnificent sunset.

Cat glanced behind her to see that she was on an isle with a concrete fort. As curious as that was, her main focus was Fintan.

She turned back to him. The wind whipped her hair about her face as she started toward him. She walked fast until she was about five feet behind him. Then she lost her nerve.

What if he didn't want her anymore? What if he could never forgive her? What if he'd already bottled up all his feelings again?

That thought stole her breath. She put a hand over her heart as if she could stop the pain. Now that he'd opened up to her, she wasn't going to let him sink back into numbness and feeling nothing. She was going to prove to him that she was worthy of him—and that she needed him.

"Fintan."

He stiffened before slowly looking at her over his shoulder. "What are you doing here?"

"I wanted to see you."

"Go home," he said and faced the sea once more.

His rejection hurt, but she deserved no less. "I probably should. I know that lying to you was the worst thing I could've done, especially after how close we'd become."

"I don't blame you for that. You had valid reasons, as I've already mentioned."

Those words should've given her hope, but he still wouldn't

look at her. "My grandfather tried to tell me to let him die, but I wanted to save him. I stupidly thought I could outsmart Bran. You warned me, and I didn't listen. I lost the two most important men in my life today—my grandfather, and you."

She wiped at the tears that had begun to flow. "You showed me your heart, and I returned the favor with deceit. Humans make mistakes. I made a huge one, but I want to make it up to you."

Cat waited, hoping he would show some sign that he was listening. But there was nothing. Yet she wasn't going to give up. "I'll do whatever you want because I can't be without you. I don't want you around for protection, Fintan. I want you because I need you. You see ... I did something I never expected to do. I fell in love with you."

She had hoped for a declaration from him also. What she didn't expect was silence. As if he hadn't heard a word she'd said.

Cat wiped at her tears. She was too late. He'd already rid himself of his emotions once more. But she couldn't make herself turn away. To leave would mean she'd given up, and she wasn't ready for that. Though she didn't know what else to say that might change his mind. Ever.

The kind of love she felt wasn't the kind that could be cast aside in a week, a month, a year, or even a decade. It was the kind that lasted an eternity.

She had seen into his soul, and he into hers. That had to count for something.

Determination now driving her, she walked to stand in front of him. When she saw his eyes were closed, she hesitated. Until she saw how fast he was breathing and how his hands were clenched at his sides.

He'd heard every word. And his feelings were still there, which meant she had hope. And she clung to it with everything she had.

"I love you," she said. "I'll say it every day for as long as it takes for you to believe me. I love you. I love you. I love you."

"Stop," he said through clenched teeth.

She smiled because she'd gotten through to him. "Never. Just as I'll never stop loving you, touching you, or kissing you."

His lids lifted, and he looked at her with his red-rimmed white eyes. "Please stop."

"Why?"

"Because I can't keep ignoring you."

She reached up and touched his face. "Would it be so bad to give in?"

"That's the problem. I already have."

A laugh of joy bubbled up. She couldn't stop smiling or crying.

"It's just that I ... I'm afraid to say the words," he said.

She rose up on her tiptoes. "They'll come in time. I see them in your eyes."

"Do you?" he asked as his arms came around her, pulling her tightly against him.

"Oh, aye."

"I don't know what to do now."

Her heart ached for everything that he'd missed out on and all the misery he'd been subjected to. She was going to make it her mission to show him the other side of things each and every day.

"Follow your heart. Nothing you can do will be wrong."

"I'm not so sure of that," he said uncertainly.

She sank her fingers into the thick locks of his white hair. "You're a Reaper and a warrior. Trust yourself. Now, what do you want to do?"

"Kiss you."

Her heart missed a beat as desire curled low in her belly. "I'd like that very much."

His head lowered, but just before their lips met, he pulled back. "Will you stay with me, Cat? Is that why you came here?"

"I'll go anywhere with you. I'm here for you."

His chest rumbled with a groan, then he covered her lips with his and claimed her mouth with a savage, fiery kiss that made her soul shout with joy—and anticipation.

The next day...

Love.

She loved him.

Him!

Fintan couldn't stop staring at Cat. Nor could he believe that she loved him. The words sounded foreign in his head. Perhaps once he got used to them, he might be able to say them.

He leaned against the doorway and watched as Cat looked in awe at one of the books River had been guarding. She asked all sorts of questions. Since the Reapers had returned from the recent battle with Bran, the mood had been light in the compound.

Or maybe it was just the addition of Cat.

Yet, on the fringes was the reminder that Eoghan was still missing.

The entire group sat together in the library, laughing and

catching Cat up on everything. It wasn't long before the conversation turned to the new information about Bran.

Cael suddenly rose to his feet. Fintan turned his head in Cael's direction, looking for Death. She stood in the arched doorway with her hands clasped together.

Her long, inky black hair was pulled over one shoulder in a fishtail braid that fell alongside one breast. She was dressed in her usual black gown.

This one had a full skirt with deep red tulle layered in. The sleeveless bodice was form-fitting with a pattern of red swirls from her waist to up around her breasts.

Lavender eyes were focused on Cat.

Fintan jumped to his feet and went to stand by Cat, but she touched his hand and gave a soft shake of her head. After meeting Death's gaze, Cat walked to Erith.

Death lifted her chin. "It seems I owe you a debt, Catriona Hayes."

"Cat," she corrected. "And no, you don't."

"It's by your will alone that I'm not dead," Erith said.

Cat shrugged and said, "It seemed wrong to do as Bran asked. Even if he hadn't killed my family, I still wouldn't have done it."

"You also figured out a great many details that none of us had pieced together," Death said. "How?"

Cat glanced Fintan's way and smiled. His chest puffed out. He'd never been prouder of anyone than his woman at that moment.

"When Fintan told me about Bran, I knew he was the kind of man who believed he was smarter than everyone else. It's why I got him talking. He gave much away then. That's when I realized his plan was very simple," Cat said.

Erith blew out a breath. "Simple or not, many have fallen for his tricks. I'm happy to know you weren't one of them."

"What does this mean for me?"

Fintan moved to stand with Cat as he looked at Erith. "I've no right to ask, but can she be spared?"

"Spared?" Death asked with a quirked brow. "From what?"

Fintan frowned. "From your retribution. I told her about us."

"You had no choice. Besides, Cat has gone above and beyond for you and the Reapers, but most especially for me. I'll not sully that by even discussing the matter further."

Cael walked to stand beside Death. "Welcome to the family, Cat."

Fintan was ready to rejoice, but Cat was now frowning. "What is it?" he asked her.

She looked up at him. "If I'm in any way part of the Reapers, then I'm officially in Death's army."

"And?" Fintan wasn't sure what the problem was.

"Then I can't kill Bran."

Death said, "Leave him to me, my dear."

As soon as Erith turned her gaze to him and smiled, Fintan knew he and Cat had her complete blessing. He bowed his head.

To his shock, Death wrapped her arms around him in a loose embrace as she whispered, "I'm happy for you. It's time to let go of the past and allow Cat to show you all that you've missed."

She released him and stepped away. Then she turned, her gaze meeting Cael's as the two walked away. Fintan waited until the pair had disappeared before he turned to Cat and the future that awaited them.

"I like her," Cat said.

Fintan pulled her against him. "And she likes you."

"What about you?" she asked, a twinkle in her eye.

He placed his hands on either side of her head, letting his fingers sink into her fiery locks. "I love you."

"And I love you, my gorgeous Reaper," she whispered before rising up on her toes to kiss him.

Eoghan shut his eyes against the dark force. It was all around him, a living, breathing being. He'd fallen into this place, unaware of what awaited him.

He couldn't discern the beast from the shadows. He hadn't known to hide. And fighting it had only made things worse. He'd never hurt so badly before.

His entire body was wracked with agony that never seemed to end—and he feared never would.

The claw marks across his chest throbbed almost as badly as his limbs that were stretched out and bound. He suspected he was dinner, but he wasn't going down that easily.

He tried to use his magic, but it was like he no longer had any. This realm, or place—wherever he was—seemed to have stripped his magic and power, leaving him as defenseless as a mortal.

But he wouldn't give up.

He fought against the bonds at his wrists, feeling them cut through his skin until he was bleeding. It was that blood that eventually allowed him to slip one hand out. He set about untying his other wrist, but his fingers wouldn't move as requested.

It took him twice as long to free his hand and then his feet. He lifted his head, ready to flee, only to come to a halt. The dark force was approaching quickly.

Eoghan got to his feet and stood, ready to face the beast. He opened his eyes, but it did him no good. He saw something off to the side in the darkness. He wasn't sure what it was, but he knew he'd never seen it before.

With the beast drawing near, Eoghan had to make a decision. He dove to the side just as the force reached him.

Thank you for reading **DARK ALPHA'S LOVER**.
I hope you enjoyed the ending to Catriona and Fintan's story as much as I loved writing it.

If you want more Reapers, then you're in luck!
Up next is **DARK ALPHA'S NIGHT**.

BUY DARK ALPHA'S NIGHT NOW
at www.DonnaGrant.com

✦

And don't miss out on the Dark Kings series.
The next book set in Dark Universe, is **BLAZE**...

BUY BLAZE NOW
at www.DonnaGrant.com

✦

To find out when new books release
SIGN UP FOR MY NEWSLETTER today at
https://www.tinyurl.com/DonnaGrantNews

Join my Facebook group, Donna Grant Groupies, for exclusive
giveaways and sneak peeks of future books.
https://bit.ly/DGGroupies

✦

Keep reading for a peek of DARK ALPHA'S NIGHT and a glimpse
at MOUNTAIN FIRE ...

SNEAK PEEK AT
DARK ALPHA'S NIGHT
REAPER SERIES, BOOK 5

I am a Reaper—Death's weapon in the dark.

I don't question. I don't hesitate. I don't feel.

Not until Ettie.

She's supposed to be a key in our hunt for the enemy rising against us—just another life to protect. But one look at her, and restraint becomes a memory I can't reach.

She's fierce and stunning and so alive it steals my breath.

A half-Fae with a spark that calls to the parts of me that were never meant to awaken.

Every brush of her skin lights me up.

Every glance promises trouble.

Every heartbeat whispers *mine.*

Wanting her is a risk.

Touching her is a temptation I shouldn't allow.

Keeping her close?

That might be the one thing that destroys me.

But the danger closing in doesn't care about rules or the lines I swore never to cross.

If the enemy takes her, the world falls.

If Death discovers what she's becoming to me…I might be, too.

I was made for the shadows.

But for Ettie, I'll break every rule ever forged for a Reaper.

New York Times and USA Today bestselling author Donna Grant delivers a seductive, high-stakes tale of magic, danger, and a desire powerful enough to defy Death in the Reaper series.

BUY DARK ALPHA'S NIGHT NOW
at www.DonnaGrant.com

Excerpt

Inchmickery, Scotland
Mid-February

The drums of Fate beat boisterously, the rhythm unstoppable.

And unmovable.

It was the first time Daire felt that he and his fellow Reapers might very well lose this senseless war they were embroiled in.

He let his gaze wander around the room, looking at the faces within the confines of the concrete fort their group had taken over on the small isle off the coast of Edinburgh. It wasn't that Daire didn't like Scotland, but he missed Ireland.

There were always seven Reapers. He didn't know why Death chose that number when the group was created, and he never thought to ask. As executioners for Death, it was the Reapers' job to help keep the balance between the Light and Dark Fae.

A job that wasn't easy on a good day.

And they hadn't had a good day in a long, long time.

Death didn't prefer one branch of Fae over the other, which was why the Reapers were comprised of both Dark and Light. Though once a Fae accepted the position of Reaper, they ceased being one or the other—though their coloring remained.

There were two Dark in their ranks—Kyran and Fintan. While Kyran had the red eyes and black and silver hair of a Dark, Fintan's hair and eyes were white. He earned his coloring from killing more Fae than any other in their entire history. But that was another story.

Daire's gaze moved to Talin, who stood with their newest member, Neve, who also happened to be Talin's woman. Next to her was Baylon, who stood with his arms crossed over his chest, a frown marring his face as he spoke.

They'd been deep in discussions for the past hour with nothing to show for it. Daire wondered what the girls, who weren't present, were up to. It was an odd thought. Especially since the Reapers hadn't been allowed to have relationships before.

But all that changed once Bran escaped his prison realm and started his crusade to wipe out the Reapers and kill Death.

That's when Baylon fell in love with Jordyn, Kyran and River got together, and Fintan gave his heart to Catriona. Now, those women—all half-Fae—were making the fort their home. With Death's blessing.

"Daire? Are you listening?"

His head jerked to Cael, the leader of the Reapers. Daire looked into Cael's silver eyes and gave a single nod. "I am."

Daire wasn't as overjoyed as the others to have the girls at the fort. It had nothing to do with Catriona Hayes falling in love with

Fintan, and everything to do with the fact that Cat had done what none of the Reapers was able to—wound Bran.

While it felt as if they'd been fighting Bran for eons, it had only been a handful of months, but already, the ex-Reaper had managed to wreak untold havoc.

The worst was during a particularly brutal battle. A clash of magic resulted in Eoghan's disappearance to. . . . Well, that was the problem. They didn't know where their friend and fellow Reaper was, or how to get to him.

To complicate things even further, Bran was somehow syphoning Death's magic, linking the two so that neither of them could find or kill the other.

While it also prevented Bran and his army from eradicating any of the Reapers, the same held true for Bran's men. They couldn't be killed. And frankly, Daire was tired of fighting the same Dark Fae over and over.

"We have to stop whatever Bran is doing," Kyran said, his red eyes flashing in anger.

Daire blew out a breath. "The one weapon we had can no longer be used."

Fintan's white eyes swung to him. "We'll find another. Cat has done enough."

"No one is arguing that point," Talin said.

Neve's lips twisted. "But it would be nice if she could still hurt Bran."

"It wouldn't matter," Cael said. "Bran knows what she can do, and he'll make sure not to get near her."

"Or he could try to kill her," Kyran added.

Fintan's glare grew icy. "That won't happen."

"We need someone or something we can use to kill Bran," Baylon said.

Talin gave a snort. "As if we could find someone who would be able to fight him."

"We don't need to find them," Daire said. "We already know her."

There was a moment of silence as everyone stared at him, trying to figure out who he meant.

Cael gave a shake of his head as he guessed. "You seriously want to ask Rhi to help us? The Light Fae is working her own problems out."

"She's battled Bran before," Neve pointed out.

Kyran grunted in agreement. "Without us asking her. Rhi is one of the best warriors the Light has. She'll do it."

"You're assuming a lot," Fintan pointed out.

Baylon sighed loudly. "This arguing is pointless. Rhi couldn't help us even if she wanted to. Death has had Daire watching her for a long time. Death even wiped Rhi's memories of us—"

"Which didn't work for long," Daire pointed out. "Rhi remembered everything about Death and us."

"There may not have been a formal invitation, but Rhi is part of Death's army," Baylon finished.

Cael sighed heavily, weariness showing briefly. "Baylon's right. When Rhi helped us in the battle that sent Eoghan away, she all but officially joined Death's army. Rhi won't be able to hurt Bran any more than Cat can now."

Daire ran a hand down his face. They'd had one shot. One millisecond in which to end everything. But they hadn't realized Cat could deal a killing blow to Bran until it was too late. Once she was part of Death's army, like the rest of them, she couldn't hurt Bran any more than he could harm her.

It was beyond frustrating. Their options were running out.

How could they find someone who was brave enough to stand up to Bran—whose power was growing by the hour—and fight him, knowing they could die? Daire would do it in a heartbeat, but as a Reaper, he and the others didn't have that option.

"So, we find someone else," Neve said.

Talin smiled at his woman, pulling her against him. "It's not quite that easy, sweetheart."

"Perhaps we make it that easy," Fintan stated.

Kyran rocked back on his heels. "Our options are limited."

"There are Fae we can ask," Neve said.

The rest of them were shaking their heads before she finished. Neve was still new and often forgot that if a Fae discovered who the Reapers were, they had to be killed—one of the rules Death put into place to keep the Reapers a secret.

Neve rolled her eyes. "Fine. What about a Halfling."

"Many don't even know they have Fae blood," Baylon said. "Besides, few know how to fight, and even fewer would know how to stand against someone like Bran."

Daire rubbed his eyes with his thumb and forefinger. The Reapers were the most feared Fae of all, and they couldn't kill Bran. But if they didn't do something soon, Bran might just find a way to end Death and send everything into utter chaos.

It was a fekking mess of gargantuan proportions. And he really feared there might not be a way out for them.

He felt someone move closer to him and glanced over to see Cael.

"You look as though you've given up hope," Cael said in a low voice so the others couldn't hear.

Daire dropped his arm. "I've spent the last months veiled while following Rhi. I've learned a great deal about the infamous Fae and her connections to not just the Dragon Kings, but also Ulrik and the Dark."

"You speak of Balladyn."

"Her lover and the new King of the Dark." Daire's stomach turned just thinking about it.

The only thing that made it better was knowing that Rhi and Balladyn were in the midst of an argument and not speaking.

"I've spoken with Con."

Daire jerked his head to look at Cael, reeling from the news. "You spoke with the King of Dragon Kings? When?"

"When Talin appeared on Dreagan land, I knew we'd have to let them know of our existence. Then Rhi told them about us. It was time."

"And?" Daire pushed, needing to know more.

Cael gave a half-hearted shrug. "Con doesn't trust us. Yet. But he'll be a good ally once I prove to him who we are."

"And how are you going to do that?"

"We," Cael corrected him and met his gaze, smiling. "We'll do that. It's going to take all the Reapers."

Daire had to admit, Cael was right, but then again, he usually was. It was one of the many reasons he led them.

"We're going to find Eoghan," Cael stated loudly into the lull in conversation.

All eyes turned his way.

Cael then looked at each of them. "We're going to stop Bran. We are going to win."

"Damn right, we are," Talin said with a nod.

Each of them agreed until only Daire was left. He faced Cael and said, "We won't stop until we've achieved it all."

A small frown formed on Cael's brow. "We'll pick this up shortly."

"What's wrong?" Baylon asked.

Cael turned his gaze to Daire. "Death wishes to talk to Daire and me."

The words barely registered with Daire before Cael put his hand on him and teleported them to a small isle in the middle of a body of water. The sound of distant bagpipes told Daire they were still in Scotland.

"Come," Cael urged.

Daire looked back at Cael to see a Fae doorway. He quickly followed and stepped into another realm, one that took his breath away with its beauty.

Thick foliage surrounded him as the scent of flowers drifted around them. A profusion of melodies from the cornucopia of birds filled the air like a symphony.

His gaze moved upward to see trees towering above them. He spotted some of the brightly colored birds flitting from limb to limb, while others soared upon the currents, weaving between the branches as if dancing.

Daire slowly followed Cael along the narrow path before them —and came upon the flowers. They were everywhere, in every shape, size, and color. Butterflies, bees, and dragonflies flew about, taking no notice of anything but the multitude of flowers laid out before them like a feast.

"Where are we?" Daire whispered.

Cael looked over his shoulder at Daire and grinned. "Death's realm."

If anyone had asked Daire to describe where he pictured Death living, it wasn't this. Then again, he couldn't imagine her anywhere. He'd known she had a realm, but he always thought she just existed in the space around them.

But now that he stood among the flowers while listening to the birds and the hum of bees, he realized this suited her. Death took so much life, but she surrounded herself with other kinds.

Daire's head swiveled from one flower to another as he continued trailing Cael. It wasn't long before he spotted a tall white tower looming before them. Daire couldn't wait to see what was inside. No sooner had that thought filled his mind than Cael came to a stop.

Daire peered around him to find Death squatting beside a bush with her voluptuous black skirts around her as she fed grass to a rabbit.

"Thank you for coming," Erith said without looking up.

Cael moved to the side so Daire could better see. His gaze landed on a thick curtain of blue-black hair that hid her face. Unsure of why he'd been summoned, Daire remained silent beside Cael, taking everything in.

Finally, Erith stood, the movement of her full skirts making nary a noise. She turned to face them and clasped her hands before her while lavender eyes landed on him.

Daire swallowed. The first time he'd met Death was when she offered him a position as a Reaper. It was rare to see much of her after accepting. That was Cael's job as leader, so Daire was a little apprehensive about why she wanted him there.

He glanced at the black gown that hugged her upper body all the way up to her neck, leaving her arms completely bare. Her beauty was unparalleled, and there were no words to even begin to describe the loveliness of such a being—nor did he presume to try.

"Daire," Erith said. "You've been a great asset to the Reapers. Not once did you complain when I sent you to follow Rhi. You did your duty as I requested, and went even further by protecting Rhi on several occasions."

He began to worry that this was about him talking to Rhi. "You erasing her memories didn't work," he began.

Death held up a hand, silencing him. "I didn't have Cael bring you here to berate you. You were brought here because I wish to know if you want to continue following Rhi, or if you would rather return to your fellow Reapers to fight Bran."

Daire considered each option carefully. "Rhi is special. I know why you wanted her followed. She's stubborn, loyal, at times reckless, but amazingly brave. Rhi has several paths open before her, and it's anyone's guess which one she will take. Her power is . . . fathomless."

"Something the Light Queen doesn't need to know," Cael said.

"Rhi is careful," Daire added.

Erith patiently waited for him to continue.

Daire drew in a deep breath and slowly released it. "I feel as if I can call Rhi a friend. She's still irked with us right now, but that will change. Ever since Eoghan's disappearance, I feel . . . like we're losing. Neve has been an asset we needed."

"Eoghan will always have a place with the Reapers," Death said. "He was one of the first. And he will always be a Reaper."

That alleviated some of the worries that had been bothering Daire. And it made his choice easier. "With Eoghan gone and the threat of Bran increasing, I belong with my brothers and sister."

"Then that is where you shall be." With that, Death turned and walked away.

Daire watched her before looking to Cael. "Now what?"

"We return to Inchmickery."

"To continue tossing around ideas?" he asked, not hiding his irritation.

Cael led the way back through the dense foliage, pushing aside huge leaves as he did. "Actually, I've got a plan."

Excitement burned through Daire when he saw Cael's grin. He stepped through the Fae doorway, leaving Death and her stunning realm behind, ready to get started on this new plan.

BUY DARK ALPHA'S NIGHT NOW
at www.DonnaGrant.com

GLIMPSE AT THE NEXT DARK UNIVERSE BOOK

BLAZE, DARK KINGS SERIES, BOOK 11

His strength, his masculinity brought out something primal within her. In his arms, she felt like the Amazon warrior she'd once pretended to be as a little girl.

Anson is a fierce Dragon King, a dragon shapeshifter born and bred to protect his own. But when a rogue tech company hacks into their world, he must join forces with the unlikeliest of allies: a human female. Her name is Devon Abrams. A rising star at the firm, she has no idea that her boss is in league with the sinister Fae and their secret war against humanity. If Anson gains her trust, he can defeat the enemy from within. But first he must fight his own attraction—to this exquisitely beautiful mortal...

Devon loves her job at the firm. But sometimes she wishes she could find a man—a real man—who isn't threatened by her success. When she first meets Anson, she's overwhelmed by his powerful masculine presence and disarmingly gorgeous smile. But when he reveals his true mission—and his ability to transform into a dragon—she's irresistibly drawn into an epic battle between humans and immortals, magic and technology, danger and desire. Anson vows to protect her from the Fae. But can he control the flames of passion that blaze within his heart?

BUY BLAZE TODAY
at www.DonnaGrant.com

ABOUT THE AUTHOR

New York Times and *USA Today* bestselling author Donna Grant® has been praised for her "totally addictive" and "unique and sensual" stories.

She's written more than one hundred novels spanning multiple genres of romance including the bestselling Dragon Kings® series that features a thrilling combination of Druids, Fae, and immortal Highlanders who are dark, dangerous, and irresistible. She lives in Texas with her dog and a cat.

www.DonnaGrant.com
www.MotherofDragonsBooks.com

facebook.com/AuthorDonnaGrant
instagram.com/dgauthor
tiktok.com/@donnagrant_author
bookbub.com/authors/donna-grant
goodreads.com/donna_grant
pinterest.com/donnagrant1

www.ingramcontent.com/pod-product-compliance
Lightning Source LLC
Chambersburg PA
CBHW011151190726
48288CB00010B/3267